Kakwasi Somadhi writes with painful honesty and joyful exuberance. Her prose is alive with compassion, and her uncommon empathy is her gift to us. Embrace her words, and feel embraced in return.
— Ryan Boudinot
The Littlest Hitler & Misconception

Coming Forth by Day is a poignant and ambitious novel about one woman's courage in the face of unspeakable injustice. Kakwasi Somadhi writes with compassion and authority about the revolutions, small and large, that give meaning and purpose to our lives and times.
— Aimee Liu
Author of CLOUD MOUNTAIN,
FLASH HOUSE, and FACE

Kakwasi Somadhi's brilliant work, *Coming Forth by Day*, engages the reader with well crafted story, memorable characters, and a clear understanding of how relationships are both static and kinetic. Ms. Somadhi's writing is fresh, captivating us, bringing us along to sort through tragedy and triumph, opening us to question. Unforgettable.
— Teri Riendeau Crane, *We Never Used the F Word*

Coming Forth by Day is an extraordinary Bildungsroman delivered by three voices that reveal several intriguing mysteries. Somadhi has not only crafted an accurate depiction of the period, but the period is a central character in the novel. As we watch Loretha mature into a capable, confident, and effective revolutionary, we long for some sense of a reprieve for the characters, but, as in life, our choices (and circumstances) have consequences that limit our freedom and joy.
— Heather Hutcheson
Professor, English Department,
Cosumnes River College

The novel Coming Forth by Day is an excellent read about love, community, the civil rights and black power struggle of the 60's, and unethical medical research. I found myself captivated by Loretha, the main character, whose courageous search for healing, love and place transported me along with her journey of self-discovery.
—Gerri Scott
Counseling Faculty, Sacramento City College

Coming Forth by Day is a powerfully conceived narrative told against the backdrop of the tumultuous Sixties. Wilborn Layton General Hospital, aka the General, is the story's biggest character, casting its shadow over the life of a young African-American child struggling with a debilitating disease. It's in the General where Loretha is first offered immediate relief from her pain, an illusory salvation, from a research physician who uses her and his other patients as blind subjects in dangerous and cancer-inducing drug research that stretches over many years. In the end it's Loretha who triumphs. The fact that this novel is inspired by the experiences of the author's aunt accentuates the artful skill Kakwasi has brought to bear on this poignant story of personal heroism pitted against professional betrayal.
—Victoria Nelson
Author of *On Writer's Block*,
Gothicka, and *Vampire Heroes.*

Coming Forth by Day

ॐ

a Novel

by Kakwasi Somadhi

∞ INFINITY PUBLISHING

Copyright © 2014 by Kakwasi Somadhi

ISBN 978-1-4958-0139-6

Printed in the United States of America

Published October 2014

INFINITY PUBLISHING
1094 New DeHaven Street, Suite 100
West Conshohocken, PA 19428-2713
Toll-free (877) BUY BOOK
Local Phone (610) 941-9999
Fax (610) 941-9959
Info@buybooksontheweb.com
www.buybooksontheweb.com

Dedication

For my Aunt Bea, whose courage and tenacity in the face of lifelong illness inspired me to write this book. For my sons: Kumbufu, Steven, Devindra, Curtis, Olubajo and Ayinde; for my big extended family—the Somadhi clan, the McCombs, and the Masons—may my humble literary offering inspire us to live our dreams, write our stories, and tell them to each other and the world.

Acknowledgment

I deeply appreciate all those who advised, encouraged, and mentored me through the writing of this book and patiently waited for its publication. Included among them are the Frances E. Williams Artists' Grant, S. Pearl Sharp, the Goddard College MFA Program, Blue Nile Press, and too many colleagues, family members and friends to name here. My wish is that all writers are fortunate enough to have supporters like you by their side.

Part I

&

September 1977
Puerto de Vida, Mexico
Loretha Remembers

Chapter 1

"Carnaval de Califa!" Loretha was aroused from sleep on the first morning in Puerto de Vida by the smell of hot, brewed coffee and baked muffins, and by the distant shouts of barefoot youngsters playing in the alleyways behind the shops in town. She had read enough about Puerto de Vida and its mythic queen, Califa, to know that children were the village messengers. Their frolicking would announce that the time had come for the droves of tourists from other lands to laugh and cavort in ways they wouldn't back in their home countries. Later, a tall, black, seductively clad woman masquerading as Califa would leave her hillside cave and dance through the streets, throwing flowers and candy to her devotees.

The town of Puerto de Vida was small and rustic with cottages for meditation and rest. People from the North would visit throughout the seasons to slow the pace of their lives and re-create themselves for the world they planned on returning to. Except every September. The *carnaval* spanned three days of Mardi Gras–like carousing when people showed up from everywhere to have a good time in the name of Califa.

Loretha sucked in the aroma of cooking food, absorbed the noise of the world outside the cottage walls, and imagined that Puerto de Vida and its queen welcomed her. The notion gave her permission to have as much fun over the three days as her body and vitality could stand. Then with her eyes still closed, she winced. If she didn't have a good time, it wouldn't be bad health restraining her. It would be the thoughts about fate, how it shaped her, and how she shaped it. It would be the uninvited sightings she'd get of hidden love and suffering her friends brought along with them to Puerto de Vida, their private anguish that she began to glimpse when she could no longer hold on to her own secrets.

There were seven of them: CJ and Dolores Bernard with their toddler, Malakia; Professor Verna Mae Howard, known to Loretha and the world as Professor Howard, and her close friend, Roy Adams—and Loretha, with her soul mate, Solly. They caravanned from Desert Haven, California, to Puerto de Vida to slip away from their roles as activists and organizers, and for Loretha and Solly, the trip was a modest honeymoon. For the elders, Professor Howard and Roy, whom the young couples had come to view as their mentors, it was an opportunity to play at being youthful again. All wanted to escape the call of social duty they'd assumed in their daily lives. They wanted to just laugh. Just joke. Just make love. Just get drunk and eat a lot without having to guard how they looked to the public, without having to watch their own backs.

Loretha moved her legs from under the blanket and onto the floor, then reached for her cane that stood propped against the bedpost. It was always by her side now, like a third leg. She wrapped her fingers firmly around the handle, and a glint of light from the sun shining through the curtains enhanced the sparkle of the lone diamond in her wedding ring. She was euphoric about the ring and what it symbolized. At least one of her wishes had come true. Solly told her, "We ought to get married, Loretha, before we go to Mexico." That's how he proposed. As unromantic as this pronouncement was, she had no desire to hold out or act coy. They'd been through too much together over the years, and besides, it was a known fact between them that she wanted to be his wife as well as his woman.

"I'm gonna need a new dress," she said, in the same matter-of-fact tone the proposal was delivered in.

"Naw," he said, "your gold outfit. You know ... you look good in it, baby."

She thought they sounded like an old couple, happily married for years, planning to renew their vows while they still could. The wedding was just as nondescript the proposal had been, a ten-minute ceremony in a chapel downtown in the big Southern California city they called home. She just had one requirement as she and Solly searched the phone book for a place to finally make their union legal: that it be nowhere near Wilborn Layton General Hospital. But they didn't go alone. CJ and Dolores, who over the past three years had become their best friends, went with them to be the witnesses.

The cook in the kitchen was Solly, and she knew he heard the bedspring creaking and her cane thumping on the wood floor, and she expected he'd appear in the doorway. He did.

"Good, you're up," he said. "The parade is starting in a couple of hours. CJ and Dolores are already out … said they'd hold seats for us in the stands. Professor Howard and Roy have left for town too."

Loretha frowned as Solly scanned her body, his eyes surveying her up and down and finally settling on her face.

"I'm fine," she said, knowing the reason for the inspection.

In the time it took for her to step forward, he swept his hand gently across her back, and then stood aside for her to pass and head toward the bathroom.

For her, grooming had ceased being a quick routine and had become an orderly ritual, one she insisted on performing by herself for as long as possible. It required her full attention so she didn't drop things or leave personal items out in the open. Still, if she kept her eyes focused on the actions of her hands, her thoughts could travel, revisiting the highs and lows of her life, which she did often.

"I'll yell if I need you," she said.

Chapter 2

Loretha was six when she first encountered Wilborn Layton General. Enwrapped in wonder, she surrendered part of her small self to it, marveling at how it reached up toward the sky and spread out over the land at the same time. The year was 1947, and after that first visit, the General became as much a part of her life as school and church. Before entering the halls of Wilborn Layton General, she'd never been inside a hospital; she wasn't even born in one. That's because the only hospital in Nettle Creek, Alabama, where she was from, didn't accept black patients. She came into the world on her grandfather's farm, arriving late, well past the date the midwife told her mother, Fannie, to expect her first child's birth. When the time came for Loretha to crawl, she did that slowly too, and it wasn't long after birthday number one that her folks realized she had weak legs and would be slow to walk. But years would pass before they knew what exactly ailed her. The best they could do in Nettle Creek was to take her to Bell Junction for a visit with Doctor Renfrow, the Native American doctor. He told them what to do.

"Get your baby girl away from here," he said. "Take her down to Atlanta to that colored medical school. The doctors there will find out what she has."

But they never made it to Georgia, because World War II emptied Nettle Creek of all its young men, sending them overseas, her father included. When the war ended and he returned, the family packed all their belongings and joined that long stream of black immigrants that moved from down South to out West looking for a better place to live, where Henry could find work and they could get medical treatment for Loretha.

Although she was quite young when they left, she never forgot the details of the trip. Her father held her hand or carried her when she tired of walking. Her mother carried her little brother, Henry Jr., born after their father left for the War. Junebug, she called him, lingering on the sound of the *e* and singing his name. The family fled Nettle Creek and rode by bus for miles to a neighboring city to catch a train heading west. And the train took them as far as it could, to Southern California, where it didn't rain much and there were no hurricanes or tornadoes. They settled in Desert Haven, a working-class neighborhood nestled — sleepily at times and restlessly at others — on the south end of the city, only fifteen miles by bus and trolley from Wilborn Layton General Hospital.

It was at this hospital where the name of what ailed Loretha was finally revealed. As a child she learned to say it—*ah-tha-it-is*—and it began burrowing its way into her identity just as stealthily as it burrowed into her bones. Loretha came into the world afflicted with juvenile rheumatoid arthritis. She saw her mother cry when the doctor told her how serious it was. He used words they had never heard before, and he talked so fast that her mother struggled to understand. Later, she overhead her parents talking, saying she had an old-folks disease and would have it all her life.

Twice monthly, and more often when her knees and ankles swelled, from the time she was six until her eighteenth birthday, she and Fannie would go to the General and sit for hours, waiting their turn to see the doctor. They learned to take sandwiches and drinks, books and games. Sometimes Fannie took her embroidery, and in the winter, a quilt to wrap around Loretha's legs.

"This is a charity hospital," her mother told her. "If we couldn't come here, God only knows how we'd pay for all this medicine and treatment you need."

Each morning before school, Loretha swallowed child-sized pills for the arthritis with a gulp of milk. Minutes later she held her breath and swallowed a teaspoon of cod-liver oil to guard against catching a cold or the flu, squeezing her eyes shut and shivering as the thick, slick, fishy liquid made its way to her stomach.

"That's my good girl," Fannie would say. "Now breathe."

Afterward, Loretha would stick out her tongue to receive her reward, a piece of peppermint candy to end the morning's ritual. When she was too sick to go out, the pain would sap all her energy, and she wouldn't hold her breath. The oily liquid would come exploding from her mouth in a geyser, mildly tinged red by the color of the pills. Then she'd have to sit on her father's lap and endure feeling her mouth held open by his strong hand while Fannie shoved the oil down her throat and quickly followed it with a spoonful of sweetened orange juice. With the ritual over, they'd wait and watch while Loretha slept or watched them as they watched her.

In 1959, when Loretha turned eighteen, her folks thought she was old enough to manage the doctors, the nurses, and her medical routines by herself, so Fannie stopped going to the hospital with her. Besides, her parents told her, since she was about to be a student at Del Rio Junior College, she had to learn to handle herself with a whole lot of strangers they would never see.

At the General, Loretha learned to adjust to the constant changing of doctors from one month to the next. She was fortunate if she had the same doctor three months in a row. She realized after a while that many of them weren't quite doctors but medical students, and some were just as afraid of the sight of sickness and suffering as they were willing to help the afflicted. She'd watch them, searching for the reason they kept their distance, refusing to look directly into her eyes unless they were shining that little flashlight into them. Sometimes they'd come to her examination room in groups and poke and talk about her like she was a lab specimen. But every so often one would break from the pack, venture a smile and a few friendly words, and call her mother Mrs. Emmitt as if their lives mattered.

Wilborn Layton General stood straight up on a hill, as if it and the hill had been crafted together from one mass of earth: man's monument, white and other worldly; nature's monument, green with tall palms spiking from it, lining the street winding up to its doors, the street that even bore its name—Layton General Drive. Separated from and towering above the flat-topped buildings on the avenue below, the General commanded and got respect.

For a lot of folks in Desert Haven, when the General's name was invoked, sometimes "going up to" would be left unsaid and only "the General" remained.

"Where you going?"

"The General."

"Why you going there?"

The answers, of course, would vary. Maybe someone had no money for a private doctor and relied on the public for help. Or maybe an old wing was being renovated or a new one added to make room for the growing number of patients from the south side's burgeoning population, bringing the promise of more jobs. In the early morning hours, men would drive up and park at the foot of the hill and walk to the construction site looking for the boss.

"Hear the General is hiring day laborers," they'd say.

Later in the day women would step off buses or be dropped off by men driving cars—women dressed in their modest business best, who were headed up to the hospital employment office.

"Hear the General is hiring clerks," they'd say.

Then there were the sick, those who had to be in the hospital and not just visiting it. They rested on metal-framed beds in wards on the upper floors, and a half-dozen patients shared a room. Metal rods holding muslin curtains hung from the ceiling over each bed. The curtains were musty green and faded from being laundered hundreds of times, yet the smell of medicine lingered in their folds. Their purpose was to bring a semblance of privacy for each patient, yet talk could be heard through, over, and around them anyway.

"What you in for?" someone would ask.

"Got the sugar blues, might lose my leg," could come the response, as good a reason as any.

"Going under the knife, huh? The General will take care of you."

"Pray for me."

"Will do."

It was built in 1909 in a busy country California town destined to become a sprawling, crowded city in just a few decades. The grateful town named it after the wealthy benefactor who gave land and money for its construction, Wilborn Layton III, real estate speculator, oil tycoon, and retired army general. The structure came in separate pieces, stacked on long flatbed wagons drawn by work horses, and erected—placed at attention—by dozens of men working in military precision.

When complete, the building was brick, fire red with rounded, arched doorways framed in gray stone. It was five stories tall and held forty beds for the sick per story. Small, but so was the city in those days.

It stood near the invisible border separating the well-off from the poor, the colored from the uncolored. It became two things as soon as its doors opened. To the folks on the affluent side of the border, it was a respected institution of medicine and research. To the folks on the poorer side, it was both tolerated and despised as a symbol of oppression. Most black folks lived on the south end of town even then, in Desert Haven, and were pushed farther south to leave plenty of room between them and that fine building. People came from miles around to this two-hundred-bed marvel. But no people of color were allowed in it except janitors: no blacks, no Mexicans, no Chinese or Japanese, and no Native Americans, that is, until the missionary workers convinced the hospital board to set aside beds for people who weren't white or didn't have much money. The missionaries won a small but significant victory.

That's the history of the first Wilborn Layton General Hospital. Decades later, construction workers piled up tons and tons of dirt that became a hill and the site of the second hospital. Then they erected thick steel and cement walls in front of the original brick building until it was hidden and dwarfed by massive stone and glass rectangles jutting up from the ground. The new construction was more than a building. It took on a life of its own and proclaimed itself with a name chiseled into its façade: the Wilborn Layton General Hospital and Medical Center.

That army of builders managed to complete the second General in 1928, the year before the Great Depression pummeled the country to its knees and threatened to bury it. The once noble brick infirmary, later called Old Red, became the hospital annex for a few years. By the time Solly was born in the General in 1939, it had become a research and teaching hospital, had given up some of its segregated ways, and everybody regardless of money, race, or ethnicity was getting treated there, even though they may not have liked the kind of care that came with the treatment. For by that year, too, the General's reputation for being a stern, mean, and cold place to have to go for some healing was in full bloom. "'Colored Only' Signs Gone, but Basement Ward at The General Still Reserved for Nonwhites," read a 1939 editorial headline in a Negro newspaper. Two years later, 1941 brought another change to the General: war, and a group of newly trained medical doctors headed off to Asia, Europe, and North Africa. That event, too, was reported in the same newspaper, for among them was Claymore E. Bernard, MD, the first black physician trained at the General, and father of the yet-unborn Claymore Jr., "CJ."

Old Red became the jail ward.

Chapter 3

The day she met him was extraordinary, and it happened a few months after her twenty-second birthday. Dr. Claymore E. Bernard walked into Loretha's exam room at the General and held out his hand.

"Hello, Miss Emmitt," he said.

He smiled. He looked directly at her and smiled. Loretha remembered everything that happened at the meeting and on that day. It revealed a lot of information about the General. She repeated Dr. Bernard's words in her mind. Miss Emmitt, he had called her. In all the years she'd been going to the General, twice monthly year in and year out, she could count the number of times a doctor or nurse had called her Miss Emmitt or her mother, Mrs. Emmitt. Fannie, they called her mother, especially Nurse Mumford.

It was puzzling, too, coming as it did on the same day a shooting rattled the whole world. It was too much drama happening all at once. She wrote about them both in her journal that night and out of respect, she wrote about the shooting first.

Nov.22/63.

Something scary happened today. They shot him. Just like they shot Lincoln, they shot Kennedy. They really do kill presidents. You trust you're getting the truth about Lincoln's death in history books, yet somehow it still seems unreal. But here it is again. This proves it. Now watch. Somebody crazy will get blamed. Booth was crazy, wasn't he? Dead presidents. Hard to believe.

Dr. Bernard propositioned me today, I mean, invited me to do something. I have to think about it because it's one more thing that seems unreal. He called me Miss Emmitt too. I almost don't believe that either.

She started her day preparing for her visit to the General. First, she took her medicine. Then she turned the radio dial to the Johnny Otis show and began moving her feet in time with the music just as the song beckoned her to do. Next, she heated the hot comb on the stove for her morning hair ritual and took care not to burn her scalp and ears as she pressed out the kinks. For this, she had to stop dancing, contenting herself with humming along freely. At least she didn't have to worry about her father interrupting. As soon as she heard his car in the driveway, she turned the radio off. She didn't want to listen to his fussing about how young ladies with college degrees didn't bother with that kind of music, especially first thing in the morning.

Then static abruptly replaced the music. She reached to tap the radio with her hair brush and heard her mother scream. At the same time, the blare of civil defense horns began cutting through the air, putting Desert Haven and the whole city on security alert.

Fannie had a streak of fear run through her that she never bothered to hide when faced with a crisis, and she didn't change that morning. She talked about how she didn't know what the Lord was trying to say by letting a good man like Kennedy get killed. She kept asking what was in store for colored folks with him dead, as though Kennedy had been the second coming, no less, and had gotten killed all over again. Loretha knew her mother's fright would have to run its course, but she felt it was her duty to try calming her all the same.

"Mom, it'll to be all right. We'll make it through this," Loretha said.

She even reminded Fannie that somehow colored folks survived after Lincoln was shot. But Fannie had an answer for that too. She said she couldn't recollect anybody ever saying what colored folks did to get by after Lincoln died. And it made no difference either way.

"It's the devil's work, that's all. And you can't tell me folks don't have cause to be scared," Fannie said.

Loretha had liked Kennedy too, and couldn't understand why anyone would want to kill him. To her the assassination was more than the killing of one man. Something else died with Kennedy. She just didn't have words to name it, but she knew that Fannie felt it too. This puzzle was at the root of her mother's fear even if neither of them could name it. She was glad when her father came home. Fannie was so upset she didn't even want Loretha to keep her appointment at the General.

"Why shouldn't she go?" Henry said. "The world won't stop turning because he's dead. White folks will see to that."

Loretha continued getting ready, all the while listening to her father explain himself.

"Of course, I don't feel right about the president getting shot," he said.

She heard her mother crying and knew by the shuffling sound of house slippers over the hallway linoleum that Henry was leading her into the living room. There he'd hold her, talk to her, and try to calm her down.

"I know Loretha told you everything will be all right, didn't she?"

"Yes, but," Fannie said, "she just like you. Both ya'll say everything's fine no matter what's happening."

"She's right, you know."

Loretha guessed what was coming next. He'd remind Fannie about the march on Washington back in the summer. They had watched it on television, and Fannie was afraid then too, thinking that with all those black folks in one place at one time stirring things up, trouble was bound to happen. Henry longed to be in the middle of things, but he couldn't take off from his job. Loretha cut pictures of the event from magazines and newspapers and hung them on the cork board out back in Henry's work shed.

"Why don't you stop all that crying, honey, and come on in the kitchen and have some breakfast with me?"

Loretha finished dressing and left the house in such a hurry that she forgot her cane and had to go back for it. Almost missed her bus.

Everybody talked about it at the General. Even Nurse Mumford chattered away, telling Loretha how pretty the first lady was and how nice she looked in those little hats.

"You'd look pretty in one of them," she said, handing Loretha a hospital gown.

That was the first time Nurse Mumford had ever given her a compliment in all the years she'd been going to the General. As the years passed, Loretha watched Nurse Mumford's straight blond hair turning white and noticed the fine wrinkles around her mouth growing deeper, and she wondered if time had begun to soften the aging nurse.

That was when this new doctor walked in and introduced himself, and Nurse Mumford left the exam room. She'd never done that before. Loretha put one hand behind her back to close the flimsy gown, clutched it tight, and placed her free hand across her midsection, just under her breast.

This doctor didn't have on a long white lab coat. He wore a black suit and a gray tie like he'd just come from a meeting and was going to another as soon as he was done with her.

"Don't be nervous," he said. "I won't bite."

Loretha took his outstretched hand cautiously, noting that his smile seemed warm and yet fixed, as if it was always present even when no one was looking and ready when someone was. She mentally pulled her father's words from the list of do's and don'ts he had planted in her mind for situations just like this one.

"Always look strangers in the eye, 'specially if you're doing business with them. When they're friendly, you be friendly. When they're serious, you be serious."

She could see her father's face silently mouthing his instructions as she tried to decide which situation the new doctor in a business suit presented.

"I'm Dr. Bernard. How are you today?"

"I'm fine, sir. I mean, I feel well," she said.

She quickly put her arm back in its place across her midsection and kept clutching the back of the gown. He was silent as he sat down in the chair across from her, still smiling, placing her chart on the metal utility cart next to the exam table.

"I guess you must be wondering what this is all about," he said, folding his hands on his lap and leaning forward.

Loretha's expression didn't change. "Yes, sir," she said.

"Actually, I'm not in the clinic often. I don't see many patients because of the other work I do. That means I can get to know my patients a little better. Loretha held her caution close, noting his easy tone, how he paced himself, pausing often, as if he were sipping a drink—scotch over ice, maybe, like her father drank—taking his time. She kept expecting Nurse Mumford to knock twice on the door at any moment and open it quickly to usher in a few medical students to watch Dr. Bernard demonstrate how to be a physician with her as the example.

"Nurse Mumford tells me you're a student at Del Rio College. How are your studies going, Miss Emmitt?"

"I graduated last year, sir."

Snatches of the tension between her and Nurse Mumford flashed forward. It was a memory Loretha would have loved to erase. Nurse Mumford asked question after question until satisfied. Loretha wanted to tell her to mind her own damn business but she wasn't raised to talk to her elders like that.

"Yes ma'am, this is my fourth semester," she remembered saying to Nurse Mumford. "I'm majoring in business communications with a literature minor. Yes, ma'am, my grades are good. This book? Greek mythology. I have to read it for world lit."

She became sullenly quiet as the nurse said she couldn't figure out why any teacher would make students read a book that old.

"Frivolous, a waste of time, especially for you people," the nurse told her.

She looked Dr. Bernard straight in the eye like her father told her and wondered how Nurse Mumford got along with him, since he was black and Nurse Mumford did not seem to like black people that much.

"Two-year colleges ... fine places," he said. "My wife takes classes from time to time at Bayside College. What's next in your future, Miss Emmitt?"

She gave him a snippet of the answer she'd mentally rehearsed for situations like this one, for strangers, older people trying to decide if she's worth their attention.

"I'd really like to go back to State, get married, and have a family if I can."

As she spoke to the doctor, her thoughts formed a picture in her mind reminding her of how much she wanted to be free of aches and pains and how much she wanted to be like the other young women who left Del Rio and made their way to State. The picture stirred her desire to belong to somebody special, somebody with a car, and he'd blow the horn to get her attention. He would stop just long enough for her to bounce in quickly, and he'd smile and wink at her approvingly. His girl, her guy. It reminded her of how much, really, she wanted to be loved, to have a boyfriend hold her and not think she's so fragile he couldn't hold her tight. She wanted to go out dancing without that cane around to slow her down. In spite of all she had endured, the medicine, the needle pricks, and the pain in her legs, this yearning stayed with her like a companion chained in place, then he spoke and the sound of the doctor's voice brought her attention back to the room.

"A good education, a husband and family … Those are good things to set your sights on. You deserve them," he said. "Everybody deserves a chance at happiness, especially a bright young person like you."

As he spoke, he shifted in his seat so that the glare from the ceiling lights cast a green glow over his brown skin, causing his eyes to shine like dark amber, the kind that could reflect images in a wavy, distorted fashion. She wondered how she looked to him, or if he really saw her at all.

"So the arthritis doesn't keep you from getting around, I see."

"It slows me down, sir. My ankles and knees get tired and swell if I stand or sit too long."

She hesitated for a moment and then said, "But that doesn't stop me."

"Good to know, Miss Emmitt. You're a very strong young woman."

"Thank you, sir."

"Has anyone talked to you about new developments in arthritis management, especially surgery?"

"No, not really," she said.

His question was surprising. She'd gotten used to one doctor asking questions and scribbling on her chart. Then a different doctor would come along, look at the chart, and ask the same questions she'd heard before, scribbling away just like all the others. Yet the questions, and the answers, never changed her treatment. Her illness and chronic pain were being managed, and she was kept alive and functioning. But this question was new.

"Well then, I'm sure there must be something you want from life, something you can't get, really, because of the arthritis. I can help you with that."

She noted how he stopped talking to wait for her reaction, and she realized she was being examined, that Dr. Bernard's questions were dancing around a theme. The dance was the examination, and his eyes saw more about her than she could see about him.

"Help different from what I'm already getting? What kind, sir?"

He hesitated. "Research, Miss Emmitt, very promising. It will change your life. I believe it is ground-breaking," he said, pursing his lips, savoring the taste of that drink she imagined him sipping.

The word "research" intrigued her. She knew what it meant in academic terms. "Careful study," trips to the library, long hours poring over books and articles for papers she had to write. The objective was discovery—her discovery, her enlightenment. His research had to be different. It was science. Real science, not the classroom textbook stuff she experienced at Del Rio. She did okay in those classes too, but they didn't prepare her for this. Bernard was standing in the doorway to a world she never imagined existed, enticing her to enter.

"We've developed new drugs for arthritis that'll ease your pain and slow the damage to your body. There is one major hitch, though."

Loretha waited for him to explain, her eyes registering the question she did not ask.

"I'm in charge of a study, and we need people, especially young people, Miss Emmitt, to join us. There's a good deal in it for you. All the treatment you need and no long waiting. It begins with minor surgery on your knees."

He smiled in that fixed way when he said this, then looked at her knees and tapped them lightly with a rubber-tipped instrument. When he looked toward her face again, she sensed that he was looking for her reaction or that he saw through her and knew how she felt. Her heart beat a little faster and her mind raced toward a word he hadn't spoken—cure—and the thought brought a vision with it. She saw herself walking, strolling, even strutting, without that third leg, her cane, tapping right along with her.

"I don't have any way to pay for new treatment, sir. I mean, no insurance, and my folks can't afford to borrow money."

"You don't have to worry about cost, Miss Emmitt," he said. "That's all taken care of."

"This study, uh, treatment, is it experimental?"

"Yes," he said. "But we've come a long way, and I wager you'll see a big change very soon after starting. That is, if you agree to join the study."

His words held a promise and placed a choice before her, enticing her with a seductive risk that clouded her ability to inquire and to do her own research. She couldn't think to ask why she was chosen. She couldn't think to ask why he was interested in the disease that crippled her, and why he needed especially young people. She didn't yet know how to question authority as big as his. That would come later, much later. With this offer before her, she could think of only one question, and she followed it with an implicit wish.

"What's the risk, Dr. Bernard? I mean, will it really help me live better?"

"There is virtually no danger, not anymore," he said. "Anyway, you'd be closely watched. In the unlikely event a problem crops up, I'd take you out of the study. On the other hand, if you come on board, you'll be one of the pioneers, helping yourself and others too."

"I need time, sir," she said, "When do you want my answer?"

"You have a clinic appointment in two weeks. It would be good if you gave me your decision by then. If you have questions in the meantime, feel free to call."

He held out his card to her, and she took it, freeing her arm from guard duty across her chest and letting the skin under the gown breathe again. For Loretha the card was another first. She stared at it briefly and then at Nurse Mumford, who had entered the room.

"Thank you," she said. For the brief time the door was open, she watched him step out into the hallway, seeming to move Nurse Mumford out of his way with just a look. Her thoughts followed him and she imagined him sauntering smoothly out to the parking lot and driving away in a fancy sports car, red or silver or one of those new copper-toned fast jobs. Freedom, she thought. Power. And then a question: research?

On her way out of the building, she watched her reflection in the glass doors and instinctively stretched her slim body to stand as tall as she could, to look proud, to focus on herself and the offer Dr. Bernard had placed in her path, right on the crossroad between life as it was and life as it could become.

She sat down to wait for the bus and wondered how her folks would see it. A good thing? The answer to a prayer? The devil playing with her life? She placed money in the fare box and took a seat behind the driver. As the bus lurched forward, she thought again about the image of herself in the glass doors and how much that self wanted to be normal. She longed to be like the young, pretty college co-eds whose pictures she saw in *Ebony* and *Jet*. She wanted choices that seemed out of her reach. She thought about letting her hair grow longer and straightening it more often and wearing flashier earrings. She wanted to make people focus on her face when they looked her way and not on what was below her waist. She sighed and her eyes wandered to the tip of her cane. Yes, Dr. Bernard, she thought. Is there a reason not to say yes? What is the reason?

She wanted yes to be right. Yes.

Chapter 4

She accepted Dr. Bernard's offer and felt free almost immediately, but the exhilaration came checkered with patches of anxiety. She was pitifully naïve and didn't know how complicated freedom could be. Should she tell her folks? How much should she reveal?

Initially, she planned to tell Mamie, her best friend, but she could never find the right time. That's because Mamie was in love and about to get married. She'd be making wedding and honeymoon plans and Loretha would be disclosing information about research and places in the General she didn't know existed. That is until after she signed her name on some papers Dr. Bernard's assistant handed her, swearing she was of sound mind and understood what she was agreeing to.

Her first real act of liberation from her folks was silence, but only after fretting over how to tell them and playing around with not saying anything at all.

Her mother would look for something religious, a sign, and she'd want the whole church to pray over it before giving Loretha her blessing. She'd have everybody listening for a message from the Bible or looking for a vision reaching out from the baptismal scene on the wall behind the pulpit at Old Ship of Zion Baptist Church. The sign would have to be as clear as water from a well, and Loretha would be reminded of it every time she set foot in church.

She knew her father would be just as hard to deal with, perhaps even more so. He had a problem with World War II, and the promise of freedom and democracy he had put his life on the line for while overseas. When the war ended, Henry returned to his hometown of Nettle Creek, Alabama, and found nothing had changed. A black man was still called *boy* or *uncle* and a black woman, *girl* or *auntie*. Whenever Henry and Fannie left the farm and went into town, they still had to step off the sidewalk to let a white person pass. And then there were the black soldiers who would turn up beaten or killed if they had trouble settling back into the feudal rituals of the Southern way of life.

Loretha grew up hearing stories of the family's journey by train from Alabama to California and how they settled in Desert Haven. Henry had tasted freedom on the war front, even in the middle of all that fighting, and Nettle Creek couldn't hold him down any longer.

She was used to seeing her father wear his veteran's status like a badge, unable to release his rage over unresolved injustices he experienced before, during, and after the war. At every chance, he'd challenge people in authority or whose social position was higher than his. She figured he'd want to meet Dr. Bernard, question him about his credentials and his research, and if he didn't like what he heard, he'd argue and then he'd call a family meeting to talk her out of getting involved.

Loretha didn't want to risk missing her chance to be normal like other young women because of her father.

But she wished she could tell her brother, Henry Jr. Junebug she called him still, even though he was a grown man. She figured he probably wouldn't hear her though, even if she got the chance to tell him. His lust for drugs was so ferocious he had nothing of himself to share with anyone else. Besides, she'd have to find him. She would have to put word out on the street for Junebug Emmitt to get in touch with his sister.

She thought of telling her folks slowly. But then she sifted back through the years, looking for times when she talked about her visits to the General, the times since her eighteenth birthday when she started going there alone, for instances of something she said about a doctor or a nurse, and she couldn't remember any. Even telling them of the research in small doses would be unusual, and they'd suspect something strange in her actions. Small bits over a long time might work, but telling them anything about the research right then wasn't a good idea.

There is no easy way to do this, she thought, no easy way to let them in and no easy way to keep them out. The right moment to tell them a tidbit arrived on a Sunday afternoon in January of 1964, three days before the scheduled knee surgery. She was setting the table for dinner. Her father sank himself into the sofa and stared at the black-and-white television, watching his favorite basketball team struggling to stay in the lead. His usual weekend bottle of scotch, bowl of ice, and the Mason jar he drank from were arranged on the coffee table in front of him. Her mother was in the kitchen listening to the *Gospel Hour* on the radio and dishing food into bowls for Loretha to place on the dining table. They had just that afternoon heard from Junebug. He said he was calling from Old Red where he had checked himself in for drug treatment. Even though it was Junebug's third time down that road, the atmosphere in the Emmitt house was so warmed by the news that her father opened a window to let in some of the cool January breeze.

"Glad you're getting yourself off the streets, Junior," she heard her father say. "Maybe the third time will be the magic charm for you."

"Praise the Lord," Fannie said.

This is it, Loretha thought. Now I can let out some of what's going on with me. She waited until the phone call ended and her father had settled back into the game. Fannie was already seated at the dining table.

"Speaking of treatment, I'm going up to the General Wednesday morning for knee surgery. I'll be back home Wednesday night, won't even have to stay in the hospital."

The other team tied the score, throwing the game into overtime. Her father yelled at his team for letting the play happen and then turned the TV down and looked at Loretha.

"'Retha, did I just hear you say surgery? How come you just now telling us?"

"Well, you know how the General is," she said.

"New doctor. Minor surgery. New procedure. Says it will cut the pain. Know what? Says I won't need my cane as much if everything goes right."

"Same day, huh?" Henry said, as he took his seat at the table. "Want me to pick you up before I go to work? Unless, of course, you got somebody else coming for you."

Then he began blessing the food as he did every Sunday, his cheeks glowing red and shiny and emitting their own heat, and his speech slowing down from the scotch he'd been drinking all afternoon. She didn't even have time to respond.

"Father, we thank thee for the blessings you have bestowed on us today, for the nourishment our bodies are about to receive, for the good news from our son who battles to find his way in this world full of temptation, and for our daughter. Bless the doctor's hands so they move in perfect harmony with thy will. May our Loretha come from under that knife whole and complete and ready for all the goodness you have in store for her. Amen."

"Amen," the two women said in unison.

Loretha picked right up where the conversation left off before the prayer.

"No, Daddy, I haven't asked anybody else. I was planning to ask you," she said.

She was aware of Fannie eyeing her with a half-quizzical, half-pleased look.

"Loretha, baby," she said, slowly chewing her food, "I'll send in a prayer request for you. I know you forgot to do it, least I didn't see you put no paper in the prayer box this morning."

Loretha nodded, knowing there was no way to get around the gossip her surgery would stir up among church folks, but at least the talk would happen after it was done, not before, not when all the good wishes and the fearful warnings from the nosy and the well-meaning might slow her down.

She was ambivalent about deceiving her folks that way, yet relieved that she managed not to reveal the whole story. It wasn't the first time either, her stretching the truth and omitting some of it when it came to telling them about her business. When she finally explored her feelings in her journal later that evening, it wasn't ambivalence or relief that fascinated her. It was the power of the secret.

Wednesday came. Loretha rose early, dressed, drank two cups of tea, and stuffed a pad of paper, some writing pens, and a novel she'd just started reading into her canvas book bag from college: Michener's *Hawaii*. She hoped by the time Henry picked her up at three she'd have at least the first hundred pages read. After all, she wasn't going to be anesthetized for the surgery. Only the feeling in her knees would be deadened with shots of nerve-numbing chemicals. She'd be alert, listening to the doctors and nurses talk, and sensing their hands and fingers on her flesh. And she'd be alert afterward, resting in the recovery room for a few hours while the attendants watched over her and checked for signs of an allergic reaction to the drugs she'd been given.

"The initial injection in your legs will hurt," she was told, "so we will give you a topical anesthetic to ease the pain. The needle prick will feel like a pinch, that's all."

Loretha knew there would be some pain, and she decided on her way to the General to endure it by thinking about how her life would be different from that day forward.

"When you are nice and numb, we will insert medicine directly into your knees to help your body to regulate the fluids that nourish your joints."

The surgery began. Loretha listened as long as she could to Dr. Bernard explaining the procedure to his assistants before her imagination drifted away to that island paradise of Michener's novel. Bernard made a small incision on the side of each knee. He inserted a tiny bubble filled with a powerful new steroid, so new it had no name. The bubble would dissolve over time, he told her, spreading the steroid gradually into her bloodstream, rebuilding her bones, preventing further deterioration of her muscles, and lessening pain and swelling. After that, no further surgery would be needed. She'd simply take more of the medicine orally, in pill form, the way she'd been accustomed to practically all her life.

Mom and Daddy are uneasy about this, she wrote later. *But they will get over it when they see how much better I'll be.*

She remembered a warning from Dr. Bernard shortly after the surgery, when she had gotten used to seeing him in the lab instead of the clinic.

"Most people have a love-hate relationship with medical research," he said.

It was on the same day she saw two men dressed in special hazard clothing rolling metal boxes strapped to a large hand truck down the hall. She paused momentarily and watched them, wondering what was so dangerous that they had to dress like they were going into outer space. After all, she thought, nobody wears anything special when they wheel the dead down to the mortuary.

She was silent as she watched the men disappear through large doors marked "Danger, Keep Out."

"Probably research contaminants, perhaps infected lab animals," Dr. Bernard said, in answer to Loretha's question about the men and the boxes.

"That's too bad," she said.

"Too bad? What's bad about it?" he said.

"It seems cruel. Animals are used up and killed."

"You make it sound downright evil," he said. "It's not a bad thing at all, believe me." He stopped checking her ankles and knees for swelling and looked directly at her.

"Cruelty isn't the intent," he said. "Yes, it is a sacrifice. Think about it. Lab animals are given over to a greater cause. Where would we be without them?"

His choice of words prompted her look at the idea of sacrifice from a different angle. She thought of the usual ways she heard the word invoked. People sacrifice for their families, for their country, for a cause they believe in, and for love, the kind of selfless giving that brings honor and respect and maybe even more love. But she'd never heard people talk about sacrificing themselves for medical research. She had given herself over to it. She'd made a deal with Dr. Bernard for something in return. Was that sacrifice or just a gamble? "Miss Emmitt," he said—he still called her that. "Let me caution you. People mean well but they don't understand research. They object when they learn humans and animals are used, but they want the benefits all the same. Not a good idea to talk too much about it. You'll get asked questions you won't know how to answer."

The question about sacrifice slinked to a corner of her mind, but slowly like it didn't want to go. She bargained with it, almost pleading, asking it to wait for an answer, to wait its turn, assuring it that an answer would come, by and by. For now, she thought, research is more important. Research, her secret.

Chapter 5

Loretha and Solly left the cottage the first morning in Puerto de Vida and joined their companions to watch the parade. Although the day was young, a festive mood had already taken over the onlookers. Some tourists and villagers standing near the sideline danced and bounced to the mixture of African and Mexican drum rhythms, and Loretha began to wish she had visited Puerto de Vida when her health was good and she could still move about. She imagined herself standing on the sideline dancing along too. That's when her thoughts left the parade and she saw the years starting with 1963 streak through her mind and stop abruptly in spring 1968.

By then she was busy being a grown up woman in a research project, involved in important stuff. She had years of medical logs she kept faithfully, meticulously, the way Dr. Bernard's assistant had shown her. She wrote on loose-leaf notebook paper divided vertically down the center, storing the sheets in three-ring binders, one for each year she'd been in the study. She stashed the binders for past years in a box under her bed. The binder for 1968 stood upright on the floor, wedged between the nightstand and the wall behind it.

She wrote in the log every day. On the left side, she named the medicine she swallowed, the time, and the steps she followed. She'd take her temperature and pulse rate an hour before and an hour after ingesting the medicine, and she recorded those numbers in her log too. She had to follow each step of her routine in precise, consistent order, and any deviation from the routine as well as the reason for the variance had to be recorded and called in to the lab.

On the right side of the page, she described how her body felt and any new pain or swelling and its location. Over time, she recorded feeling less and less pain. She noted any new signs of an allergic reaction like nose bleeds or rashes, and soreness anywhere on her body and sometimes no new symptoms at all. The truth was that Loretha had gotten along so well during those five years without hurting and with fewer symptoms, that if it weren't for the logs and hospital visits, thoughts of her disease wouldn't have crossed her mind at all. Her cane, gathering dust as it hung on a hook attached to her bedroom door, went unused for weeks at a time.

She'd save her feelings about the research and the General for her journal, the few minutes a day when she'd shine a light into the caves of her mind and explore what she found there.

She couldn't get over seeing the General as cold, even though things in the research wing were different from those in the main clinic. In the lab, people seemed friendlier, less hurried, more willing to look her in the eye and smile. They called her Miss Emmitt. If somebody called her Loretha, it was because they were known by their first name too, like Julie. Even when Julie phoned Loretha to check on how she was doing with her medical routine, she'd simply say, "Hey, Loretha. It's me, Julie. How are things going?"

The General is stand-offish. Like it can't do its job if it gets involved with the spirit of folks who come for help.

Those words entered her journal the same day the General stirred up trouble with the media, the public, the board of supervisors, and the city council for letting a man die in one of the outpatient waiting rooms. He'd been sitting there all day. Nobody realized he was dead until time to close, and the security guard couldn't wake him. The story made the newspapers and reminded Loretha of the scene she'd witnessed when she left the hospital the day she met Dr. Bernard. She saw a pregnant girl, in pain, rocking back and forth on the plastic bench in the waiting room. She was alone, no husband, no boyfriend, no mother or sister. *Where are your people?* Loretha thought. A nurse yelled at the girl as if she thought the pain had interfered with that poor child's hearing.

"It's not time yet. Come back when your labor pains are five minutes apart. How did you get here?"

Loretha hastened her steps toward the exit, hurrying to get away from what she was hearing.

"No, can't go back there," the girl said.

As Loretha reached the exit, the words "Are you on welfare? We'll have to call your social worker" trailed out into the daylight with her.

She'd heard stories about babies being born in the waiting room, and she wondered if that's what happened on that day. There was little help for the girl rocking herself and her unborn baby, and none for the man who died while patiently waiting for somebody to come to his rescue. Yet, she thought, there was an offer of real help for her. These ripples from the past made her wonder about the randomness of it all at the General, where help was not supposed to be a matter of chance.

She didn't know these words were hiding out in her mind until they flashed on the pages of her journal and surprised her. They told her something else she hadn't thought about until then, that she worked for the General. She had to put her pen down and soak in their meaning, the unspoken facts and the hints seeping from under the covers of her pact with Bernard. She thought again about sacrifice, and now she had her answer. This was no sacrifice, for she was on the payroll.

I work for that place, just like I work for the library around the corner from my house. Only all I give the library is my time. I give the General my whole body and it makes me feel normal in return. That's my pay.

Labor troubles always nagged the General too, and Loretha watched a line of union workers picketing for the right to organize the janitors, year in and year out, it seemed to her, for as long as she'd been going there for her treatments.

The day she met Norah, the picketers changed and so did their messages. They were younger, louder, and some wore white, green, or blue clothing resembling medical scrubs. They carried signs that said, "Health Care is a Right" and "Affordable Health not War."

One day she saw a man with signs made of white poster board covering the front and back of his body, held over his shoulders with cord. The front sign asked the question, "What Grand Old

Man spends more for war than health?" And the back sign answered: "Uncle Sam that's who."

Once again, she thought she ought to read up on the health issues demanding her attention every time she went to the General. But as soon as the protestors were out of sight, they were out of mind. She'd let the thought slip back into a corner somewhere in one of her mental caves, refocusing her attention, her light, on something else more pleasant, anything that wouldn't remind her of the pact she'd made with Bernard and the General.

Meeting Norah showed Loretha that trouble wasn't the only reason people got together at the General. She was sitting at the bus stop reading a book when a young woman in her midtwenties rolled up in a wheelchair. The woman announced herself and asked what Loretha was reading. Then she said she thought they were in the same research project because she had seen Loretha coming from Dr. Bernard's lab one day. She was really glad to meet somebody else in the study. She laughed when Norah said Dr. Bernard's icy personality could suddenly steam up if the subject was research. He was always defending it against an ungrateful public.

Loretha was reading *The Heart is a Lonely Hunter* because she had seen somewhere that Richard Wright had called it a great book. Loretha discovered that Norah had read the same book a few years earlier and loved it. But Norah had never heard of Wright, so Loretha told her about *Black Boy* and *Native Son*. As they sat waiting for their rides, they talked more about books and writers and, in between, they eased into talk about the research.

"How long you been in?" Norah said.

"January, '64. What about you?"

"Eleven years. I was fifteen when my folks signed me up."

"That's a long time," Loretha said.

Loretha and Norah became friends. The illness living in their bodies linked them, so did the research holding their hopes for a cure, and so did their love of books. They exchanged phone numbers, but realizing their calls would be long distance, they decided to write each other between visits.

Loretha got together with Norah as often as her own schedule and her friend's transportation arrangement allowed. The two would sit in a corner of the cafeteria or on the patio in warm weather, and read and talk until Norah's mother came for her. She would arrive in a big station wagon, old, with faded yellow paint, and Loretha watched from a distance as the older woman helped her grown daughter into the car and loaded the wheelchair into the trunk. Then they'd drive off to a suburb forty miles west of the hospital, and Loretha would catch the bus back to Desert Haven.

Her friendship with Mamie changed in the years between 1963 and 1968. They were still best friends in Loretha's mind, because their shared history—the migration of their families from Nettle Creek to Desert Haven—had kept Loretha and Mamie close as they grew up even though their personalities were opposite. Loretha was laid back and bookish and Mamie was outgoing and popular. All through high school they had talked on the phone every night. In college, they still kept close, studying together, taking in a movie or going shopping as often as their young adult lives allowed. They kept close even when Mamie left Del Rio and made it up to state a whole year before Loretha. They kept close even when Loretha dropped out of State after one semester because she had such a struggle walking between buildings to get to her classes on time. Once she even found herself locked out of an exam for being late.

It was Mamie's marriage that changed things, for after she became Mrs. Norris Lee McCombs the communication between Loretha and Mamie slowed. Before the marriage Loretha would even go on occasional blind dates with some of Norris's single friends, but the dates stopped altogether after Mamie and Norris became Mr. and Mrs. However, Loretha didn't believe that Mamie had deliberately dropped their friendship but just needed time and space to build her life with Norris. Anyway, Loretha figured Norris's friends were probably going into the military, which Norris did as well in 1966.

Loretha landed the part-time job at the library around the same time her dream of getting a four-year college degree evaporated, just before she met Dr. Bernard. She looked at the job as a kind of consolation prize. She had a knack for staring back at her disappointments and looking for signs of opportunity. After all, she did have an associate's degree, and the library would accept her degree plus four years of experience in place of a bachelor's degree for some of its professional positions. She figured she'd make a career of it and move up in the system. That's the hope she wrote in her journal, plus the forced quiet of the library fit her personality. She loved the idea of being around all those books.

That plan worked out fine for a few years, until the county announced it was suspending all new hiring and closing some neighborhood libraries to save money. The branch where Loretha worked was unfortunate enough to make the hit list. Of course, community leaders protested, so every evening, as punishment, Loretha thought, she'd have to call in the day's statistics to the main library downtown: how many people came in, how many checked out or returned books, how many new cards were issued, how many folks came in to use the public typewriters or reserve the community meeting rooms.

One slow evening after Loretha had just finished her daily report, the phone rang and she answered, even though the library had already closed. It was Mamie.

"Wait for me," she said. "I'll be there in ten minutes to pick you up."

"I'm pregnant, and Norris is getting sent to Vietnam after his training."

They sat in the back, away from the dinner crowd at Ella Jay's Soul Food Stop, where they had spent a lot of time during their college days at Del Rio. Loretha figured the least she could do was treat her friend to a meal, but food wasn't on Mamie's mind. Loretha saw that Mamie was in a panic and needed somebody just to listen. They drank tea, and Loretha nodded and sounded alarmed while Mamie talked about what scared her. If Norris didn't come back from Vietnam, she'd have a child to bring up alone, and she didn't know how she'd support the baby and herself with him gone.

"Maybe you can move back in with your folks," Loretha said, "just for a while."

"They're talking about going back down South. They never really took to the big city, too much concrete, too many bright lights, stray dogs, and sirens for them."

This new development in Mamie's fortune signaled a change for Loretha as well. Her lifelong friend may have to leave, and the miles and circumstances separating them could turn them into strangers. For once, Loretha didn't envy Mamie. She left Ella's that evening with a deeper sense of what they meant to each other, and she felt an unwelcome shift in the landscape of her life. She asked herself if there was something she could do to slow things down, something to ease her friend's troubles, but her mind couldn't conjure up an answer.

What Loretha had envied most about Mamie was her worldliness. Mamie graduated from State, landed a job paying good money so she could move away from her folks, bought herself a car, and stayed on top of the latest fashions. And she did it all before deciding that Norris would be the man she'd marry, which rendered her, in Loretha's eyes, the epitome of a free woman. What's more, she was black, which made her success all the more sweet.

At twenty-seven, Loretha was as bound as Mamie was unbound. She still lived with her folks. She wanted to move out, but the issue of money stopped her. She didn't have enough to afford a place by herself, let alone a car and some fine clothes. The evening job at the library actually caused her to lose money. Since her high school days she had earned money tutoring: first, her classmates; then later, neighborhood kids. But her evening schedule at the library cut into the time she would normally have spent tutoring kids. Much to her disappointment, she couldn't convince any of her young clients to change their appointments to weekends, and their parents wouldn't make them.

Her freedom was her own telephone in the room she had been sleeping in since childhood. In principle, she could come and go as she pleased, but out of respect for her folks she'd be home from the few dates she had by midnight, and nobody she went out with impressed her parents enough for them to pressure her about getting married. At least that's how they acted, but underneath, Loretha perceived that mixed with their love, they saw her condition as a handicap, something turning men's heads in other directions. She sensed that they had quietly accepted that she might end up an old maid. Besides, since they didn't know where Junebug was half the time, she understood the unspoken reason they wanted her around. Her presence reassured them they'd raised one of their children successfully.

She was their anchor as much as they were hers; they were proud of her, and considered her graduation from Del Rio a family triumph. She was useful to them around the house also. She'd help Fannie cook, clean, sew, and iron, mostly for folks from church who couldn't do these tasks for themselves, and for the few working women in the neighborhood who could afford her mother's services. She'd write and type business letters for her folks, and when called on, she helped out at her

Mother's church with written documents for poorly educated elderly members. On Henry's days off, when he wasn't caught up in his union duties or the games on television, she'd hang out with him in his work shed, just talking and whittling little pieces of wood into likenesses of animals and people the way he'd shown her when she was growing up.

"Good exercise for your little fingers," he said.

When they were kids, she was the one who showed Junebug how to hold the knife and groove it gently into the wood scraps left over from the cabinets and tables Henry built and sold in his spare time. But Junebug got mad because Henry didn't spend time teaching him. By the time he reached his teens and started running the streets, Loretha had a half dozen boxes filled with her wooden creatures. Junebug told her the only thing he wanted to do with that shed was hide behind it with some of his homeboys and smoke weed. That's exactly what he did too, and was slick about hiding it. When Henry finally caught on, however, he kicked Junebug out of the house. Junebug was eighteen, and he'd drift back occasionally on Sundays or holidays and when Henry wasn't home, but he never slept in that house again.

Loretha was a practical, down-to-earth optimist. Even though her life was so mundane it bored even her, she met the spring of 1968 secretly hoping for a welcome change that would signal forward movement. After a two-year struggle, the library finally closed, but not even losing her job could dampen Loretha's hopes. She had kept her hopes up despite the troubles in the world that seeped into her piece of it, like the riots a year earlier when Junebug was arrested for looting. He said he didn't steal anything but wished he had. At least his time in jail would've been worth the trouble.

The war in Vietnam became part of her world too, taking away people she knew and bringing them back dead or maimed or sick in the soul. That's what happened to Norris a year after he left for combat. He returned and shortly afterward, Mamie hurriedly set out to drive her husband and her baby the thousands of miles to Nettle Creek, because Norris, pajama-clad and missing half a leg, jumped from their first-floor apartment window one night. Hobbling down the street, he screamed and shook his fist at a police chopper as it scoured the neighborhood with bright lights, looking for urban enemies, disrupters, and other threats to the social order.

Even civil unrest on college campuses clear across the country seeped into her world. Her cousin Shelby, a law student at Howard University, was expelled for his part in taking over the campus administration building. She hadn't seen him in years, but they'd speak to each other whenever their folks talked long distance on the phone, and they'd send each other pictures of themselves every so often. But when she heard the news of what happened to him from her folks, she sent him a little money from her savings, because Shelby's dad, her Uncle Blueford, refused to give him another dime until he got himself back into law school. He wrote back to her saying he was heading up to Canada. Getting expelled meant he'd lose his deferment, and he had no intention of going to war. She answered his letter, but her reply came back marked "Undeliverable."

Loretha had a yearning for something she couldn't quite name, a desire for something new and different, and this yearning often seemed hard to control. She recalled that during those days, her heart beat faster and she breathed harder. A buzz of life moved in her, like an electric spark struggling to ignite, making her feel hungry one moment and full the next. She needed to find a way to let it gradually light up and express itself before she exploded, and she was convinced that this was the message. Her health was almost normal; her handicap, almost invisible. She wanted to see and hear more, to do more, to stand less on the sidelines observing while life itself paraded around her. She longed to be in the parade.

The way she looked that spring in 1968 made her feel good. Most of the time she wore her hair combed back and away from her face in a ponytail. Now she began to let a mass of it fall over her forehead, forming natural bangs. She wore eye makeup too, drawing thin black lines next to her eyelashes, slanting the outer edge of the lines upward, giving her a wide-eyed, curious expression. Next, she dabbed red blush onto her cheeks. Then she'd go out into the world feeling attractive, not beautiful, but pleasing to look at, like she stood a chance of being noticed and asked out.

She felt this way when she showed up at New World Bookshop and Culture Center for a job interview, her hair freshly groomed and her makeup impeccable. It was still early enough in spring to wear a light gray winter suit and not be viewed as out of touch with the fashion of the season.

Loretha wasn't a clothes horse; she couldn't afford to be, and her tastes were good-girl modest.

She mixed and matched her clothes to make her wardrobe look more extensive, and she saved some outfits for very special occasions. The interview with the influential Professor Verna Howard was like that, a special occasion, and Loretha dressed accordingly.

She waited with three other women, each of whom was decked out in rainbow colors, and she recognized two of them from Del Rio College. One wore a short skirt and black fishnet stockings. All but Loretha sat with their legs crossed at the knee, exposing their thighs. She wished she could cross her legs like that, but even with her new freedom since the knee surgery, she couldn't do so without feeling pain after a few minutes. The best she could do was cross her legs at the ankles like the etiquette books said to do for job interviews.

She was the last to be called by Professor Howard. She rose swiftly, secured her purse strap over her shoulder, pressed the folder holding her résumé to her chest, and limped a half step with her left leg leading, before breaking into a full stride toward the professor. Her hand trembled as she reached to shake the professor's and looked up to meet the older woman's wide-eyed stare and tight-lipped smile.

"Be at ease, young lady."

Loretha hadn't realized until then how tall the professor was. Her hair, reddish-brown mixed with gray and arranged in a bun on the top of her head, made her look even taller, drawing attention to her because of her height as well as her reputation.

Loretha followed her into a large room, noting how the woman walked with a slow, deliberate strut, her left foot pointing slightly left and her right pointing slightly right. One day she heard Mamie say that Professor Howard couldn't seem to make up her mind which direction to walk in and Loretha laughed when she heard it. But now it seemed that indecision could never be part of this big woman's nature. She walked with calculated certainty, like she could turn to meet whatever came at her, effortlessly. Loretha saw why people at the college tended to move out of her way. She acknowledged them with a nod and a smile as she passed. She had the reputation of being a tough history teacher in the classroom but easy to approach on campus or in town. And she always introduced herself as Professor Verna Howard.

They sat across from each other at an enormous oak claw foot table.

"What do you like to read?" the professor said.

With this, Loretha sensed that her knowledge and awareness would be tested that day more deeply than for other job interviews. Hearing the first question brought her face to face with an expectation she hadn't experienced before. None of the other jobs she had held required her to really know much. When she interviewed at the movie theater to sit in the booth and sell tickets, she wasn't asked what movies she liked. When she interviewed for the office assistant's job at Bradley and Sparks law firm, all she had to do was demonstrate she could speak clearly into the telephone, take complete phone messages, file correctly, and make a fresh pot of coffee twice during her shift. She certainly wasn't expected to know anything about law.

Even at the library, she didn't have to show a fondness for books. She just had to know how to put them in the right place on the shelves, keep the card catalogs in order, and be nice to the patrons.

If she got this job, however, things would be different. This is a bookstore and culture center, she thought. The professor doesn't just sell books. She creates experiences around them. To work there, she realized she must like to read and must show a taste for the knowledge found in books. She'd have to speak to the patrons in respectable English, and she'd have to write like she knew how to handle the language.

"I like to read poetry and novels," she answered, "Emily Dickenson, you know, and June Jordan, Richard Wright, and Carson McCullers. I like others too, but those are my favorites."

"Like any history books?"

"Yes, ma'am, I read *They Came in Chains* on my own and *Great Moments in American History,* for my history challenge exam.

"Professor Howard," said the professor, correcting Loretha. "You challenged American history? How well did you do?"

"I scored high enough to advance to history honors," Loretha said.

She was disappointed when the professor didn't comment further on her accomplishment. Instead she was left alone to take a five-minute typing test and to edit a badly written article for the center's newsletter. When she finished, she waited patiently for the professor's return.

"Now, young lady, I've been asking all of the questions so far, is there anything you'd like to ask about the job?"

"I understand it's part-time. I'd like to know about the hours."

"Certainly. Twenty-five to thirty hours a week, off on Sunday and Monday. The job is long term, but I don't expect it will ever be full-time. Are you looking for more hours?"

"No, ma'am, I mean, Professor. Part-time is perfect. But I have to tell you something," Loretha said.

Honest. I have to be honest, she thought. She didn't want to start working there just to be let go if the professor found out about her illness and considered her a risk.

"I've got arthritis and I have to see the doctor twice a month. But if you hire me for the job, I'll make sure the appointments don't interfere with my work schedule."

"And how does your condition affect your typing?"

"It's in my legs mostly. I mean, I don't feel it in my hands nearly as much, and I had no trouble typing my own class papers."

Loretha waited while the professor silently scrutinized her typing and editing.

"You realize there're no paid sick leave and no health insurance here."

She assured the professor that the medical treatments were taken care of, and the truth of these words sounded good and gave her a feeling of smugness. She pictured herself riding the bus around to the back of the General and taking the short route through the hallways to Dr. Bernard's lab. She felt the same smugness when the research assistants, young doctors themselves, would review her vital signs and comment on how well the medicines controlled her symptoms.

After a few minutes, the professor returned her gaze to Loretha, smiling slightly and adjusting her glasses with her index finger.

"Fifty words a minute with no mistakes," she said, "and all the grammar errors corrected in the news article." She paused for a minute, still looking at Loretha's editing sample.

"I'm really impressed with how you rearranged the paragraphs," she said finally. "Nobody else understood that this article needed more than spelling and punctuation corrections." The professor stood up, signaling that the interview had ended.

"Can you start next Tuesday?" she said.

"Why, yes, ma'am—Professor Howard," Loretha said. Of course she hoped she'd get the job, but she didn't expect to be hired right then. It meant she'd work more hours and would have steady money, more than she earned at the library. With the money she'd earn from tutoring and editing on the side, she could afford to live on her own.

Walking to the bus stop, she saw four run-down houses in an abandoned field a short distance away. They were covered with ivy, creeping vines, yellow and purple flowers, all spread open to greet the faint sunlight peeping through the clouds in the overcast sky. As she neared the bus stop in front of them, she noticed their faded color, once dark green, and the molded trim of the roof, once orange, showing through the wild flowers. She thought of that unkempt field with its abandoned houses as forlorn and in waiting, as if crying out to be transformed into a gathering place, beautiful and useful, a park perhaps. The thought slipped away as she turned to face the bus lumbering toward her. When she boarded, a pleasant fragrance came with her.

The job paid enough money for Loretha to get her own place. Her folks didn't want her to move, but all she had to do was talk about the money and the time she'd save on bus trips to and from the General. She knew, however, that her readiness to move uncovered a major struggle for them. They gave her money that wasn't a loan, and her father made her promise to come home every Sunday to go to church with her mother, even though he never went, and to help cook Sunday dinner.

She heard the emphasis on the word "home" when he handed her the money and exacted the promise. He said it as if her home couldn't ever be her new apartment. Her home was the house she grew up in, the house whose walls absorbed her pain the days and nights they had sat with her, rubbing her legs, watching for negative side effects of medicine, and at the same time praying that a day would come when she'd be strong enough to live on her own. She smiled as they admitted they weren't quite ready when that day finally arrived.

The apartment was in walking distance from her new job, and it was a much shorter bus ride to the General for her treatments. Walking from her apartment to the bookshop and culture center became a special kind of freedom. The route was just long enough to work the stiffness from her legs, and on the way she imagined a speck of white that was the General off in the distance. Life was good too, because she could walk without her cane most of the time, and her knees didn't swell as much as they did before the surgery, before she became a subject in Dr. Bernard's research. She felt all grown up, finally, and that made life good.

The bookshop and culture center served as a social space for activists and intellectuals, giving Loretha the chance to meet writers, musicians, artists, organizers, and political aspirants wanting to be seen as liberal and progressive. Here, Loretha first observed groups of people of different races and cultures touching and talking to each other as if they were equals. She'd never paid much attention to that before. Even at Del Rio, she thought an unseen, unmentioned rule kept people apart. They came together only during public events like football games, dances, and assemblies, but even then, they'd separate into turfs. Turfs formed of black people here, white people there, one of Latinos, and another of Asians, together and yet apart. A cord of self-protective tension wove its way around each turf, drawing boundaries based on how people looked, dressed, spoke, what music they listened to, and what moves they made when they danced.

Loretha didn't exactly know how to react to all the race-mixing, as her parents would call it, at the center. She could hear her mother's voice telling her to call any older person of another race, sir or ma'am or Mr. or Mrs., and to address people her own age that weren't black by their first name. If they objected, she shouldn't call them anything at all. So she was confused when a white civil rights lawyer who frequently came to hear the lectures and rub shoulders with black authors at Professor Howard's book parties, told her not to call him sir.

"My name is Roy. Just call me Roy," he said. "If you don't want to call me Roy, then it's Mr. Adams, but not sir. I hate that."

He was smiling, so she didn't feel threatened, but she kept her guard up anyway, not knowing where the conversation would go next.

"Yes," she caught herself before the "sir" slipped out—"Roy."

"Good. Is it all right if I call you Loretha? I've got a daughter about your age back in New York living with her mother. She calls me Roy too."

Chapter 6

By April 4, 1968, Loretha marked the passage of her first month on the job and a week in her new apartment, all without problems. The day started uneventfully, with the breeze mild and the air amazingly free of smog.

She stepped lively that morning. On her visit with Dr. Bernard earlier that week she got some news that proved what she'd been feeling. Her blood tests showed the effects of the disease easing. She had more energy because she was no longer anemic. She'd gained a few pounds and she looked good, her skin a richer brown, her hips fuller, her legs stronger with practically no swelling in her knees and ankles. She could picture herself wearing shorts when the weather warmed, something she never wore before because her legs were so skinny.

She was itching to tell her folks. She hadn't had much to say to them when they called her from Nettle Creek where they'd gone to visit relatives. Fannie and Aunt Ora Lee were spending their time on the church revival circuit, and Henry and Uncle Blueford were on the lake drinking scotch and fishing as often as they could to avoid joining their wives. She could hear a conversation with them playing in her head. "How's the job?" They'd ask her. And she'd say everything was fine. She'd tell them she checked on the house on her day off, and that Junebug stopped by the bookstore and asked about them. He looked like he was doing okay, and he had a new job as a delivery truck driver for a furniture store.

With this news, Fannie would tell Loretha to kiss Junebug, and tell him it's from her and his dad too. Then she'd say how the General turned out to be a blessing, and how she hadn't stopped giving thanks ever since Loretha's operation.

Loretha worked through most of that day with a smile on her face as big as the welcome sign hanging over the double oak doors of the center. But at half past three, word of a shooting in Memphis sent customers rushing toward Professor Howard's library to watch the story unfold on television.

"Dr. Martin Luther King Jr. is dead, shot by an unknown assailant in Memphis, Tennessee, where he'd gone to support striking sanitation workers."

She left her station behind the counter. When she reached the onlookers, she stopped. She let her eyes search beyond them and around the library until she spotted Professor Howard sitting in an overstuffed chair staring at the television, lips pressed into a frown and hands resting in her lap. Silence weighed down with shock and disbelief filled the room. She walked in slowly and placed her hand on the professor's shoulder. Without looking up, the older woman returned the gesture, reaching for Loretha's hand and holding it.

They met that same evening, Loretha and Solly, in spring, 1968, with the city on red alert and about to explode once more. Loretha stood behind the sales counter again, when the bell over the door rang and he entered. She saw his pensive, serious look for the first time, and she likened it to the expressions she'd seen on the faces of black men all afternoon as they wandered in and out of the bookshop, enraged, threatened, and worried.

"Evening," he said. He did not smile.

She, however, wanted to smile, but just nodded, then said, "How can I help you?"

"I hear there's a rap session happening here tonight, my sister, that so?"

"Yes, but not for another half hour. You can wait in the library if you like."

"I'll browse around out here if you don't mind."

A few minutes passed, and then he asked, "Do you have Frantz Fanon's *The Wretched of the Earth*?" He was standing near the counter, turning the rack of new arrivals and looking as if nothing interested him.

"No, but it's on order. We get a lot of requests for it. If you give me your phone number, I'll call when it gets here."

Wonder what's in that book, she thought, so many men come looking for it, men with a certain stuck-up air about them, wearing black leather jackets and carrying those big lawyer-looking briefcases. She glanced in his direction. He fit the profile with the attire. His leather was tan though, and the matching cap was really a beret but he had no briefcase. Then she was moved to tell him about King's books.

"You know," she said, "if you're interested, we still have a few of Dr. King's books in stock."

She watched as he moved away from the rack and walked slowly toward the counter, eyeing other books along the aisle, saying nothing until he reached her.

"I've read them all," he said.

That's when their eyes met. He looked at her, really, for the first time, and she sensed him trying to decide whether to soften his gaze or keep his hard look, holding on to his rage.

"It seems King's good works weren't enough to keep him alive." He said this as he reached the counter and leaned on it.

"Name's Solly. Solly Baines."

"Loretha. Pleased to meet you, Solly."

"You coming to the rap session tonight?" he said. "We'll be talking about King, and where we go from here, to use his words."

His gaze had softened as he waited for her answer, with his frown easing into a hint of a smile.

"Not tonight," she said. "I can't tonight."

She spoke truth. This was not a night to be walking after dark, and as soon as Professor Howard's son Marcus came to relieve her, she'd leave for her apartment. As the bell sounded, the door opened, announcing more visitors looking for the rap session.

"Maybe next time," Solly said, moving away in rhythm with the small crowd of people.

"Maybe next time," she said, and watched him and the crowd disappear into the next room, all the while wondering if he'd ever return to the shop, if she'd ever see him again.

Loretha nodded at Professor Howard as the older woman began closing the doors to the library. She watched and listened as the professor spoke, switching her persona from academician to Earth Momma, her English from proper to down home, shepherding the crowd, invoking the code of conduct she enforced in her place of business.

"All right, y'all know the routine. Take off your caps, coats, jackets, and put them in the back of the room along with your briefcases. We're not having no surprises up in here tonight."

For the second time that day, Loretha's steps became heavy as she walked westward toward her apartment with Dr. King's book *Strength to Love* tucked securely in the outer pocket of her purse. Silence hovered over the din of the boulevard just as it had earlier over the blare of the television. She sensed the silence as an interlude, a void that would soon become full with sounds of chaos and danger.

The ringing phone inside her apartment urged her to hurry as she arrived at her doorstep. It was her folks, wanting to know if she was safe, because trouble had already erupted in Alabama where they were.

Not long after the call ended, loud explosions began blasting through the neighborhood. Bottles stuffed with lit, gas soaked rags flew through the air, bursting into flame and lighting up the night, burning everything they touched. The boulevard became one big bonfire, leaving smoking bones where there had once been struggling yet surviving businesses until the sun went down that April evening. New World Bookshop and Culture Center wasn't spared. Its whole backside became a fuming skeleton of wood and melted plaster, leaving burned remnants of books in the rubble.

Loretha lay sleepless in bed. She closed her eyes and imagined how the turmoil in the streets looked, and she listened to the wail of sirens and the stunted boom of pistols mixed with sounds of rapid machine-gun fire. The voice of the law bleated over loud speakers mounted atop heavily armed trucks, warning that anyone caught out before sunup would be arrested. More amazed and curious than scared, more anxious about what it all meant than about the immediate danger, she left the bed, walked to the window, and watched the smoking flames lick and stain the sky. Then she looked in the direction of the New World Bookshop and Culture Center and felt her eyes moistening as the brutality of what she saw shocked and saddened her. She swore to brave the streets and show up for work when day came, and to help the Professor until forced back home by the curfew.

Morning light arrived. She left the apartment carrying her cane. She hadn't thought deeply about being seen with it again, but the heaviness of the night's turmoil and the uncertainty of what she'd find at the bookshop told her she'd need it to lean on before the day ended.

Roy Adams was already there, standing close to Professor Howard, surveying the damage with her, and for an odd minute, Loretha imagined his arm around the professor's waist. The professor and Marcus looked surprised to see her, and Marcus was hurt with an ice pack taped to his left leg.

"I called you this morning, Loretha ... You all right?"

"Yes, ma'am, um, Professor Howard."

"What about your folks? They must be worried half to death about you."

"They're in Alabama. They know I'm okay. We talked last night."

These questions let Loretha know that her boss would not be Professor Howard that day. She

64

would still be Earth Momma, handling her business like one of the missionary matrons at her mother's church, putting her own pain aside and attending to others.

"Be sure to use the phone up front to call them while you are here. It's still working."

As Roy was leaving, Solly and two men came in a pickup truck, and two more men followed them in a car. They brought water hoses, shovels, and trash cans. They all wore black bands around their heads and arms, and the words "Brothers United" circled a raised fist on the front and back of their shirts.

"Professor Howard, the Southside Brotherhood is here to help," Solly said. And the men with him uttered a somber greeting almost in unison as they looked around at the damage.

Loretha stared at them, and her mind flashed on scenes from cowboy movies she watched as a child when the posse of good guys led by a rugged he-man showed up to help the innocent and chase away the outlaws so the he-man could ride off into the sunset with the girl. The plot was so predictable she and Junebug would crack jokes about it and break out with laughter. She held back a smile, not quite sure why Solly and his crew amused her. Then she looked toward Professor Howard, whose lips were pressed again into a frown. With her index finger, the professor pushed her glasses up and welcomed the men.

"Sure do appreciate your coming," she said, shaking each hand held out to her and repeating a name as it was announced: Tyrone, Roscoe, Angelo, Walt, and Jerome. "How about a couple of you fellows going over to help Mr. Leonardo? His pawnshop took quite a hit last night, and he's over there by himself. The rest of you can help Marcus."

Solly glanced at the youngest of the men, Roscoe and Jerome, and nodded for them to go. They turned, and on their way to what was left of the pawnshop, one said, "As you wish, Sister Howard."

"Professor Howard," she said. "You men come back at lunch time, and please tell Mr. Leonardo he's welcome to come for lunch too." Loretha's gaze followed Solly and the other men as they started toward the back of the building with Marcus showing the way. She noticed the professor watching, too, the men and the aura they created with their uniformed look and hard-edged frowns. And Marcus, with a big smile on his face, looked comical wearing a plaid work shirt and bright yellow rubber boots. He seemed not to mind at all that he didn't appear militant, though he executed the men's ritualistic greeting with precision, touching his clinched fist to his heart and extending it to touch each of their fists, making the shift in leadership from Solly to him acceptable in their eyes for that one occasion, and affirming a solidarity Loretha observed and wondered about.

"Real good to see you, brothers," Marcus said. "Come on back here and let me show you what we got to do."

They too labored as a team that day, Loretha and Professor Howard, working side by side sometimes or at opposite ends of the shop at others, and mostly without exchanging words. They covered their faces with scarves before sweeping away dust, soot, and broken glass. They sheathed their hands in work gloves and picked through remnants of books and memorabilia, carefully, in case shards of glass still remained. Loretha took a ruler and lifted a small, scorched, folding table from across a pile of books lying charred and soggy on the floor. "Wretched" was the only word readable on the cover of one. We did have a copy after all, she thought.

She stirred and stirred the pile, gradually realizing nothing salvageable was left and knowing the sound she heard from across the room was Professor Howard, weeping and talking softly, almost in a whisper.

"Just like Texas," Loretha heard the older woman say. "They burned papa's store. Burned up Louis too. Nothing left of him but ash to scatter in the wind."

The curfew ended, and people all over the south side and Desert Haven, still wounded, still in pain, settled into a routine of cleaning up the debris and going on with their lives. Loretha observed how quickly Professor Howard pulled herself together, pushing her chest out, lifting her glasses, and directing her eyes straight ahead. She kept right on doing as much business as she could under the circumstances. But Loretha sensed too that the professor's actions signaled more than a return to the way things were before the assassination and the fires.

"Life is always hurling change at you," she told Loretha.

It had been three weeks since the fire, and the professor was planning something big, a "still-in-business fire sale." Loretha busied herself putting sale prices on books damaged a little by the fire but still in good enough condition to sell. Some were new arrivals, delivered the day before fire.

"Small change, big change," the professor said, mumbling at times, letting her sentences trail off inaudibly.

Yes, ma'am, Loretha thought, wondering why her boss was talking to her that way or if her words were really meant for herself and she just needed Loretha for a sounding board.

Then the professor came to the middle of the aisle where Loretha was working and talked directly to her.

"And you have to figure out how to capture it, you know. Make it serve your will. You can pass out in front of it, defeated, or you can throw your hips at it, beckon it to come for you so you can get as much from the change as you can hold."

"If you don't mind my asking, what is there to capture besides the people who tried to burn down Desert Haven? I mean, don't we have to adjust and move on?"

"Well, we've already done that. What's next is to expand, build Freedom Village right next to the bookshop. We'll still sell books and have cultural events, but we're adding a freedom school for young people. That's change."

Loretha slowed down a little to take in what she'd just heard. "But what if a riot happens again?"

The professor answered with questions of her own. "Riot? What riot? That was no riot. Where was the mob?"

"But all those people out there, burning and looting. People were really mad. Wasn't that a riot?"

"Let me tell you something, Loretha," said the professor, twirling a new book rack she'd just bought.

"Think about it. There was a whole lot of order to the way those fires started, the way some businesses burned and others didn't. The looting might have been random, people running from stores with televisions and couches big enough to break their backs and getting caught on camera. But the bank? Somebody blew it up and actually got away with money. People got hurt and killed too. That poor bank guard. You know, he left a wife with a house full of kids for her to feed."

"If it wasn't random, who do you think planned it?" asked Loretha.

"Don't know, and not going to speculate," said the professor. "Don't want to use the word revolt, least not yet. Nobody's made any demands. 'Random' just isn't the whole story here."

Loretha finished with the price tags and started helping the professor arrange books on the new racks.

"But why would anybody want to deliberately set fire to New World?"

"Don't know that either. Maybe we were in the way of a cocktail aimed at some other business, or maybe we were a target but got lucky and didn't burn completely down."

"What's so important about being here?" said Loretha. Then she blurted out, "Why not move your business to a safer part of town?"

"Our business, Loretha," the professor said. "What's a safer part of town anyway? You know, I can't make a lot of money selling books and putting on cultural events, but I can make life better over here in Desert Haven. And that's all I am doing, Loretha. That's all."

She opened up to me today, Loretha wrote later.

The rebuilding and expanding began. Loretha assumed more duties, doing everything from bookkeeping and helping customers to preparing refreshments for folks coming by to pitch in. It was her idea to place a canopy in the backyard away from the construction to create an outside break space for helpers. And it was her task to keep the fruit bowls stocked, to replenish the coolers with freshly made sandwiches, and to see that the cold drinks were surrounded by plenty of ice.

She liked listening to the workers' banter when she stood under the canopy. She glanced from time to time at their backs as they sawed, hammered, painted, swept, and stomped sawdust from their work boots. When she'd spot Solly's back, she'd stop looking.

One afternoon, she couldn't find his back, and the loss was greater than she could bring herself to admit. She saw his absence as abandoning his post, and she became cynical about it. *He's always talking about what would have happened if he skipped off his post in the army. What's going to happen now that he's left his post here? Anyhow, where is he? Is he coming back?* She thought.

But when she turned to go inside, she eyed him standing next to the fence, holding a cigarette between his fingers and drinking water from an army canteen he always had with him on the job. He smiled and nodded as he lowered the canteen. Feeling exposed, she blinked rapidly and cut her eyes away from him, disappearing into the building, all the while feeling his eyes watching her.

The two-story, wooden frame, Victorian-styled house, whose rooms had been converted years earlier into a bookshop, library, and social hall, received a complete makeover. Wood siding became thick adobe, painted a deep, rich gold like the evening sun shining on desert sand. A wood-and-brick archway bridged the open space that once separated New World Books and Culture Center from the structure that used to be Leonardo's business. The pawnshop faded into the history of the boulevard and was reborn as Freedom Village.

The professor hired local artists to paint the story of people of color in California's history on the walls of her new building. And there Califa was, this time black as midnight instead of mellow brown like on the wall of the General.

With the construction complete, Freedom Village opened at the end of October just before the weather changed. Loretha addressed fancy invitations to everybody big in town to the lavish open house the professor planned. All the businesses and neighbors close by got the same fancy invitation. She wondered why Professor Howard was going to such trouble, why she didn't just have the event announced on the radio. But she soon learned what the professor was up to. The bigwigs wouldn't show up unless they got special treatment, and she was determined to give the people of Desert Haven the same consideration. She even convinced the Desert Haven Chamber of Commerce to help her publicize the event.

Loretha learned too that young folks from the area would be hired to dress up in white jackets and dark pants or skirts. They would serve the guests, and the food would be laid out on gold-rimmed china and served with sterling silver flatware. No plastic and no Styrofoam. She found herself once again blown away by the professor's knack for drawing from a storehouse of characters living inside her, how the professor knew just which one to call on, and how swiftly she changed from one character to another, like an actor changes costumes.

By the day of the grand opening, leaves had started to turn from green to the deepest red, purple, orange, and mud brown, breaking from their branches, and swirling down to merge with the earth. Autumn was showing off, bringing harvest for the new Freedom Village, bringing revival for all of Desert Haven. Folks felt lucky, like the whole town was about to hit the numbers and win big. The field languishing down the boulevard from Freedom Village, for years the blight of the neighborhood, was about to become the park Loretha imagined just a few months earlier. Loretha heard the professor announce this at the start of the festivities. She was flanked by city and county officials, ministers, local business people, and her book-loving lawyer friend, Roy. He circulated among the guests like it was his grand opening too, stopping long enough to stand by the professor's side while she spoke. Once again, Loretha could imagine an invisible gesture, his arm around the professor's waist.

"We have some out-of-sight news to bring you today," the professor said to the crowd. "Those green-and-orange haunted houses, and the weeds in that big field down the way, are about to change into something beautiful for this oft-neglected part of the city." She paused. "A park named after Martin Luther King Jr. Now tell me that's not something to celebrate."

Loretha felt even more excited after hearing the news. She felt something like a warm vapor coursing through the air and connecting the people, causing them to speak and smile and nod and touch. It was the same sensation she had felt when she watched the workers' backs as they built Freedom Village. It was slow and sweet and pleasing, like her secret vision of Solly in her mind's eye. She quietly breathed the sound of his voice into herself, and she hoped.

Loretha sat across from him most of that afternoon and evening, talking, listening, checking him out, and mentally dancing with the attraction she believed growing between them.

The way he greeted her reminded her of church, even though she knew by his actions he hadn't stepped inside a church on a Sunday morning in a long time. And she saw the greeting as impersonal, part of the front he presented to the world. He called her Sister Loretha. She even heard him call the professor Sister Howard behind her back. And she heard him call other men, young and old, brother. As much as she wanted to be in his presence, that quirk about him annoyed her.

"Sure is a good day for a celebration, wouldn't you say so, Sister Loretha?"

And she responded by following her mother's advice, calling him by his first name.

"It sure is, Solly. Are you ready to celebrate?"

"That I am. Sister Howard's got a good thing going on here."

"*Professor* Howard," Loretha corrected him.

He tilted his head up and laughed, "Oh, so that means you don't want me calling you sister? What should I call you?"

"Loretha will do."

"Why, too much like old-time religion, is that it?" He leaned toward her, winked, and whispered.

"Well, yeah. You should say that to somebody close, a member of your family or group. That's why church folks do it. Everybody's not your sister or brother," she replied. I don't want to be your sister, she thought. The emphasis in her mind was on the word *don't*.

"I only talk to black people that way, because we're united in struggle whether we go to church or not." He leaned toward her again, and whispered, "Sister Loretha."

She frowned and rolled her eyes.

They continued tugging with words at the edges of the feeling she had for him and that she sensed he had for her. She listened quietly as he made a point of letting her know why he was so hard on the church scene.

"I am without religion," he said, holding up his finger and letting his sunglasses slip down on his nose, mocking a preacher.

"Whenever the gods split the deck up evenly, I might decide to listen to them. Notice I said *them*."

"Is that why the Southside Brotherhood is moving its meetings from New Haven Baptist to Freedom Village?"

He nodded, took a sip from his wine and continued to talk.

"Freedom Village is perfect. Open to everybody, even church folks," he said. "People can say what's on their minds without worrying about stepping on somebody's god."

"So you don't start and end your meetings with a prayer?" she asked.

"Not if I can help it, and the brothers picked me to preside over things. No prayer."

"Why not?" she said.

When she said this, he looked away and the smile left his face. Then he removed his sunglasses, slipped them into his shirt pocket and gazed at her again, with a kind of quizzical look. His smile came back but only slightly.

"Your Southern upbringing is showing, girl."

She said nothing, and the heat in her started turning to anger, like she was not in a mood to be played. She sipped her iced tea slowly. The tinkle of ice against glass, click of forks and spoons against china, and the sound of voices chatting and laughing bounced against the feeling she tried to control. It was clear that he planned to ignore the question, but on that evening, she needed an answer. In rhythm with the music, he bobbed his head on the counter beat and tapped his fingers against the table, occasionally humming the highs and lows of a saxophone or piano solo.

"You like jazz?" he said.

"Some of it, sometimes," she said.

"Bet you like gospel."

"Some of it, sometimes."

She paused, sipped her tea, and munched a cocktail shrimp slowly until it was all gone. Then she placed the toothpick on the plate.

"Tell you what," she said. "I like my questions answered."

"Okay, yeah. The God question," he said. "I believe there might be a God. I mean, there must be something to it, and you know our people have staked everything they got on it. But does God bless and protect? From what? You can look around the world and see a whole lot of things God decided not to protect us from. So no, I don't pray. Do I disappoint you, Sister Loretha?"

"No. I've got questions myself, but I still pray. You've heard of 'walk softly but carry a big stick?' Prayer is my big stick. Keeps me going."

She was silent again. He kept moving his head to the music, which to Loretha seemed exaggerated, but soon she began to sense his movements were a prelude to something else, that he needed to speak. "So what do you think about the professor starting a freedom school for neighborhood kids?" he said.

"What do I think?" she quizzed. "I think it's a great idea, I'm going to be one of the teachers."

"Yeah, why?"

She looked at him puzzled for a minute, wondering if he knew of a reason not to like the idea.

"Well," she explained, "because I get to teach about my own people, and pass on information I learned here at the center instead of in school. A few kids around here might get some of this stuff on their own, but for most this will be their only chance."

She watched him out of the corner of her eye as he sipped his wine and continued to nod in that overstated way to the music.

"I have to agree with you," he said finally. "You know we're starting a black student union up at State. We'll be volunteering some time down here in the village too." "Sounds exciting," she said. "I wish I could ..." and she hesitated. "I wish I had time to take a class so I could join."

"Why don't you make time?" he asked. But he spoke again before she could answer. "What else do you like to do besides work for Professor Howard, read books, and take care of a brother's appetite for good food?"

His question caught her off guard, even though she sensed where it was leading. She even wanted to be led there, but at that moment she felt she was not good enough. For a second, she flirted with making up something to compete with other women she figured he knew, women with lives more interesting than hers.

Before she could respond, he spoke again and it was as if he knew what she was tempted to say. "It's okay, Loretha. You don't have to look for something impressive to say. I just want to know what you like to do for pleasure so we can do it together sometime." For the first time he didn't call her sister.

She guessed she'd have a companion on her walk home that evening. She was right. The weather cooled, and he slipped his jacket over her shoulders and offered his arm.

"Let's start a rumor," he said.

She locked arms with him, and he quickly slid his hands into his pants pockets as they set out walking the three blocks to her place, each wearing a smile.

"And what rumor might that be, Mr. Solly?" she asked, breaking her mother's rule.

"Loretha, please, be cool," he chuckled. "Brother Solly or just Solly, all right?"

Her attraction to Solly was another one of her secrets. The only two people she'd tell anyway were Mamie and Junebug. After all, nothing might come of it. Maybe he had someone already, a girlfriend he didn't bring around. Men were like that. They'd show up in places without their wives or sweethearts, she thought. Just as his leaving her question hanging annoyed her, the conflicting thoughts forming in her mind changed her mood from excited anticipation to mild anxiety. *He's about to ask me out,* she thought. *And he just might have somebody waiting for him as soon as he drops me off.*

"You know, Loretha," he said when they reached the steps to her apartment. "I think I jumped a little ahead of myself earlier. I'd sure like for us to spend some time together ... you free? Can you go out with me?"

Her smile returned, and she hoped it was enough to hide what she was thinking, for she was aware that he knew the answer already. He knew when he brought up the subject the first time. He was playing his part as the gentleman, the gracious brother, with the jacket around her shoulders and offering his arm.

"I'm free," she said, handing him the jacket. "But you, Solly, what about you?"

"I am," he said, looking away as he tucked the jacket under his arm. Then he looked at her. "I am," he repeated, pausing slightly between each word, penetrating and melting her doubt with his gaze. "How about Saturday after the Village closes? Why don't I pick you up? We'll go to Ella Jay's for dinner and then to the Brotherhood's movie of the week. It's a classic Paul Robeson flick. You up for it?"

She was. They said goodbye to each other and she entered her apartment, closing the door and clicking the night latch almost in one motion. She stood leaning against the door until she could no longer hear the tap of his heels and she was sure he had gone. Then she turned, and as her eyes adjusted to the dark, her reflection in the mirror sharpened and she saw the outline of her body. The image pulled her thoughts back to her condition, her legs, trips to the General, the secret, and she remembered why she welcomed Dr. Bernard's offer. She heard his words once again.

"What are your plans, Miss Emmitt? What do you want from life?" he had asked her.

She answered out loud as she walked toward her image in the mirror. I want to be normal, she thought. I want to be loved. That's what this is about. I'll take my chances.

She watched her body in the mirror squares glued neatly to the wall. The last of the evening sun's orange glow lit up the decorative gold veins that meandered through the glass, making her skin look bronzed. As she approached, she pulled her shoulders back, thrust her chest out, and stood tall to face Solly's advances just as she had faced Dr. Bernard's offer years earlier. When she reached the wall of mirrors, she lifted her skirt and stared at her legs, and from the corner of her eye glimpsed her cane, its handle peeping from behind the leaves of the elephant palm whose shadow stretched across the mirrors toward her.

Chapter 7

On the second day of the *carnaval*, children danced in the streets again to wake the tourists who had the good sense to sleep during the night, and refresh the ones who drank and partied until morning light with no intention of sleeping. By the time the Desert Haven visitors settled around a cafe table in town for breakfast, the children were running from restaurant to restaurant carrying baskets full of trinkets to sell.

"*Por La Senorita*," a boy said, greeting Loretha. He deftly slid the bow of a ribbon tied around a papier-mâché Califa doll onto the arm of Loretha's wheelchair. She nodded for Solly to buy it, thinking it would look nice on her nightstand when she returned home. The boy told her in his best English to pray hard and Califa would bless her legs so she could leave the wheelchair behind.

Amid the morning chatter of folks again ratcheting up their group spirit to a drunken pitch, Loretha wondered what secrets lurked beneath the revelry or stood naked in plain sight.

She tried to recall the various tricks she played on herself through the years to keep her mysteries locked away. The year Solly began seducing her into his world, she had defiantly ignored the thought about her secrets that crouched in one of her mental caves. It said that things hidden have a way of unexpectedly stirring, throwing the lid off the box they're locked in, and lunging out like predators onto unsuspecting prey. The thought was her intuition warning her, but she was in no mood to heed it.

In 1969, she let Solly into her life. She had been seeing him a whole year before her secret jumped out at him. The night it happened, he spotted her medicine in blue plastic boxes in the back of her refrigerator and knocked the medical logs off the top of it where she kept them between two globe bookends.

She let him in gradually, properly, the way she figured her folks would want. For a while, she felt as though she was being courted. He'd ask her out, and there were always a few days between the asking and the time they'd spend together. And it seemed to her they couldn't make it to their destination without his having some revolutionary business to take care of beforehand, and he would include her. Often his business took a while, and they'd be late to the movie or lecture or concert they planned, but she never felt disappointed. She liked seeing him lead events and persuade people, and she got the notion he enjoyed having her around to watch.

But occasionally she didn't hear from him for weeks, and just when she thought she'd been dumped and forgotten, he'd show up and tell her how busy he'd been, what was going on in the movement keeping him away, and how much he missed her. His words to her were sweet talk that elevated her womanly urges so high she struggled to keep them under cover, even when her desire for him bumped against her natural caution, and she didn't quite believe him.

Late one Saturday night, when she hadn't heard from him in several weeks, he called from San Francisco. She had been reading in bed and had barely closed the book and turned out the light, thinking she'd tired herself enough to allow sleep to come.

"Did I wake you?" he said.

Before she could answer, he apologized for calling so late and asked if he could see her the first thing when he returned to Desert Haven. He'd get there by late afternoon the next day. She told him she'd be with her folks because it was Sunday. He asked if he could pick her up at their house and if she'd go to the Brotherhood's emergency meeting with him. She didn't get an answer when she questioned him about what was happening. Instead, he told her not to worry, just a few revolutionary changes shaping up around him that's all, and everything was okay and he was lonely in the 'Frisco Bay fog without her.

Professor Howard hadn't mentioned before closing on Saturday there would be a meeting the next day, so Loretha knew Solly had to have worked things out with Marcus. If Marcus was part of the picture, Professor Howard would feel all right about people in the Village late on a Sunday night without being there herself to oversee things.

Loretha finally fell into sleep hours after he called. The part about his being lonely triggered her wakefulness, her drifts back and forth between belief and doubt, hope and caution.

The next afternoon when he picked her up and they drove away from her folks' house, she saw her parents peeking from behind the curtains of the picture window in the living room. She wondered what they thought of Solly with his big hair, thick, nappy, and clipped into a perfect circle crowning his head. It was summer, but he wore a Dashiki over a dark turtleneck sweater, and she assumed that's how he dressed in San Francisco where the weather was cooler. Her folks invited him to stay for dinner, even though Loretha had already said they'd be leaving as soon as he arrived because they were going to a meeting. Her mother wanted to know if it was a church function. Loretha said no, that it was a community gathering at Freedom Village.

"Community meeting? Can anybody go?" Her father said, pouring himself more scotch. He still drank liquor from Mason jars and still spent Sunday afternoons watching sports on television. This time, the Dodgers were in the third inning of a scoreless game. His voice sounded stern, but because he'd been drinking all day, Loretha couldn't tell how to gauge the seriousness of this threat.

"Oh, Henry, you know you not going nowhere but out there in that shed," her mother said.

Henry chuckled, his facial expression hanging between a smile and a frown as he turned the Mason jar up to his lips, all the while looking from Loretha to Solly.

"Ya'll young people go on and have a good time," he said finally.

Loretha hadn't told her folks about Solly, but Junebug knew for a while what they didn't, that she was dating a revolutionary who grew up right there in Desert Haven. She told Junebug back in the spring when he stopped by her place to show off his first car. It was a '64 Mustang, red with fat whitewalls and shiny silver rims. He'd saved enough to buy a newer car, but 1964 marked the year he really started getting his life back from drugs, and he wanted his first car and his first year clean to match up. Loretha laughed at his logic.

"Have you been by the house to show Mom and Dad?"

"Been by to show Moms. You know I don't go there when Pops is home."

"When will you two at least try to get along?" she said, almost as if she didn't expect an answer, but he responded, and quickly.

"When he stops trying to beat my butt every time he sees me. It's like he thinks I'm still a kid, and he's worse when he's drunk. And don't let him be sober and somebody mention how much alike we look. Then he starts in with the nagging, getting on my case about what I should be doing with my life and stuff. Anyways, he drinks like he's got a liquor store all to himself out in that shed."

"I know," Loretha said. "Mom says it's every day now, and he starts drinking early in the morning."

"Enough about Pops. He'll pull himself together sooner or later. What you got good to eat, Sis, and by the way," he said as he headed for the refrigerator, "who was that tall, lanky dude I saw you with down at the Limelight Lounge? When you start doing the club scene? Caught you, girl," he laughed.

Loretha looked with surprise at her un-revolutionary brother who straightened his kinks with chemicals and molded his hair into a pompadour that turned red and straight on top, and stayed nappy and black at the roots. He had survived the streets and conquered drug addiction, and he just wanted to have a good time without getting into more trouble. She wondered what the first encounter would be like between him and Solly.

"How long has it been going on, Sis?" he said.

"I've got chicken wings," she said. "I'll fry some and make waffles if you stick around."

"I'm staying, and you can throw in some of your fruit salad if you want to. Now tell me about Mr. tall-black-and-got-all-his-shit-together."

"His name is Solly Baines. We haven't gotten serious," she said. "I met him when I started working for Professor Howard."

Junebug washed his hands in the kitchen sink and started looking for ingredients for the waffles.

"He looks stone wild with all that bushy hair. Boy, I'd hate to be sitting behind him at the picture show."

Loretha laughed. They finished preparing the meal, ate, and watched television together for a while, talking some more about their folks and about life. Finally, Junebug said he'd better leave because it was getting late, and his girlfriend would be mad and not open the door when he got to her place if he waited much longer.

"Let me know if your bush man gets out of line, you hear me?" he said, as he headed out. "I might have to teach him a thing or two about how to treat my big sister."

When Loretha showed up with Solly that hot July evening, the village was already crowded. Men and women with Afros as big as Solly's came regaled down in African dashikis, flowing robes, leather coats, caps, and boots. Some women sported fine African wraps on their heads and bangles of copper, gold, and silver on their forearms. Loretha, still in her Baptist Sunday-go-to-meeting clothes, felt out of place. She was glad Solly assigned her to take notes because it gave her something to do and freed her from feeling like she was out of step with revolutionary fashion. She lowered her head, focusing on the paper in front of her as Solly announced to the crowd what her role would be.

"Sister Loretha here is gonna take minutes and mimeograph them. In-town folks can stop by the Village Tuesday and pick up a copy. She'll mail copies to you brothers and sisters from out of town."

She learned that the Brotherhood had joined forces with two other groups, one from Northern California and the other from San Diego. The three organizations planned to form a statewide coalition. After some shouting and pontificating over what to call themselves, they settled on United Revolutionary Vanguard. The argument continued well into the evening over where the headquarters would be and how to merge officers. Eventually, a fight nearly broke out over who would keep the money.

At one point, Loretha stopped writing and just listened, looking from one revolutionary to the next, trying to guess what each would say as if she were watching a movie. Finally, after she took up her pen again and began scribbling notes, she heard Marcus announce they needed to be out by twelve, and anyway Loretha had to be getting tired of all that writing.

On the ride to her apartment, Solly asked if he could keep some of his personal papers there with her, not much, just a couple of file boxes, until the URV found new headquarters. Loretha agreed because the thought of having a piece of him with her was a small victory. When she'd start having doubts about his motives, she could point to him sitting next her couch in the form of cardboard stationery boxes painted black and speckled to look like metal, with just a lid to cover their contents, and no lock. She saw the act as his opening himself more to her.

She felt so good about the prospect that when he asked if he could come inside despite the lateness of the hour, she said yes to that too.

The sun came up the next morning, shining on the freeway dust covering Solly's car, still parked in front of Loretha's apartment. She cooked breakfast for him, and as he left, he kissed her long and hard and said he'd call her that night.

It was Monday, Loretha's day off. She still earned extra money tutoring on the side, and her only obligation that evening was English tutoring with three high school students who were prepping for college entrance exams. She'd have the whole day to herself.

She went to the stove to heat water for another cup of tea, passing the open window with its curtain waving and undulating in the breeze as it had done the night before. The moving air released the scent of night-blooming jasmine still lingering in the mesh of the screen and the weave of the curtain. She breathed in the fragrance as she moved, putting away the morning dishes while waiting for the water to boil. She placed the tea bag into the cup, noting the whistling of the tea pot. As she poured water over the bag, she watched the liquid turn dark. She felt warm inside even before taking a sip.

With the magic of the night still fresh in her mind, she sat down across from the window and watched the curtain move. She closed her eyes, lacing her fingers together around the cup and let the warmth of the liquid seep into her skin. She remembered how he led her to trust him by guiding her with his hands and probing deep into her eyes with his own. It was then that she closed her eyes because she felt naked, as though he had begun to dissolve all of her defenses, he finally spoke, telling her in a commanding whisper to look at him. She held her breath and complied, opening her eyes and meeting him, and he promised not to hurt her.

She stepped out of her apartment that morning and walked two blocks down Oasis Boulevard and into Clipper Bill's Barber Shop.

"How you doing, little lady? What can Bill do for you today?"

"You style Afros for women?"

"Why sure, little lady. Come on in. What you want? Big fro, little fro, sideways fro, you name it and I can style it for you."

She followed him to a barber's chair. Two young apprentice barbers were arranging their area as they waited for customers, and she felt self-conscious knowing that their eyes slyly surveyed her body from the legs up. She looked straight ahead as if they didn't exist, following closely behind bow-legged, bald Clipper Bill. She sat down and waited while he retrieved a large, leather-bound binder, pulled up a stool and sat beside her.

"Take a look at this here. When you see a style you like, stop me."

He opened the binder and showed Loretha dozens of photographs of men, women, and children sporting professionally shaped Afro hairdos. Loretha finally saw a style she liked and pointed to it with her finger.

"That's it?" said Bill. "You got it."

She smiled and her heart thumped haltingly then fast against her chest for a few seconds as he covered her clothing with a clean gown and tucked a towel into it around her neck. Her breathing quickened as he slipped his fingers through her hair and held it up so she could see how long it was for the last time. She was about to spend the next half hour getting her hair clipped short and shaped into a V at the nape of her neck.

Her muscles tightened and she winced, closing her eyes as the electric clippers began buzzing her hair away. Clipper Bill's fingers moved swiftly, expertly, snipping with the scissors at a few stray kinks here and there, then using a brush and a hand-held dryer to blow off the remaining loose strands and give her new hairdo the smooth look she saw in the picture. When the cutting and grooming ceased, she looked at herself in the mirror, approvingly. She closed her eyes again, only for a moment, and imagined Solly cradling her face in his hands and kissing her hair, just as he had done the night before.

When she paid Clipper Bill, she also bought a can of Afro Nectar Hair Spray and a plastic hair pick. She asked what else she needed to keep her new hairdo looking nice. He told her what shampoo was best and which pomade would keep her hair soft. Finally, he told her to come back in two weeks for a touch-up just as she would do if she had gone to a beauty shop. Then he added a comment about how shameful it was beauticians wouldn't style Afros.

"You know what?" he asked, but didn't wait for her to respond. "They'll come around, you wait. Right now though, their shame is my gain."

Hair has weight, she thought, stepping onto the bus. She figured that for a time she'd miss the feel of it pulled back into a pony tail or resting on her shoulders. She even imagined herself missing the dark brown line of hair framing her face when she moved her head from side to side every morning, brushing and giving her hair that one hundred strokes the beauty books recommended. Wonder how long it will take to get used to the shortness, the nappiness, she thought.

But she found herself smiling and nodding at other women wearing kinky, natural Afros, and they smiled back. They're fine, she thought. Their look was beyond just pretty. The look was beautifully handsome and comely. She recognized herself in them, and this new view helped build her confidence, letting her know she looked just as good without long, straight hair as she did with it.

She then turned her thoughts to the next part of her quest, to buy African print fabric from the sewing shop across town in Desert Haven near her folks' house. She planned to get her mother's help to sew a new wardrobe, so she could look as if she belonged in Solly's revolution.

Three months later, she heard her medical logs crash to the floor. Solly was getting himself some ice from the refrigerator.

She was doing his work, that is, the work he assigned to her for the Brotherhood and the URV. She was typing his speech for a State of the Race Conference, the first big event the coalition sponsored. When the logs hit the floor, the notebook rings flew open, and some of the pages scattered about. She lifted herself up as quickly as she could and took her characteristic limp, more pronounced in that moment because she was in a hurry. She didn't realize until then how private those logs were. Nothing had occurred in the past to bring it to her awareness, but now she gasped and hurried to rescue that part of her being inscribed on those pages and lying exposed on the floor.

"Hey baby, I got this," Solly said, smiling.

"You laughing at me?"

"Naw, baby."

"Yes, you are!"

His next words were an apology as Loretha pushed him away so she could pick up the papers and put them back in order. She had started to cry with such force that it hurt, because her secret was there for him to see, and it seemed to her like his were the eyes of the whole world, making fun of her.

He moved toward her and she felt him reaching around her back and holding her arms so she couldn't move and then lifting and taking her to the couch and rocking her, wiping away tears with his fingers.

"Those papers ain't going nowhere, not even back in them notebooks, 'til you tell me what this is all about," he said.

Loretha cried a while longer while Solly held her. When she'd calmed down enough, she began talking.

"That's me," she said, pointing at the papers. "Arthritis ... all my life."

She told him about the research and the surgery, about Dr. Bernard and Norah, and her twice-monthly visits to the General. Finally, she looked at him and met his soft stare, the way he looked when he was about to enter her.

"I don't like ... I hate telling you all this."

"Why you hate telling your man?"

"My man?" she asked.

"Yeah, Loretha, I'm your man, right? You got somebody else?"

"There you go again," she said as she drew away.

"Say it, Loretha," he whispered, pulling her back. "Say Solly is my man and I am his woman."

She sat sucking her lips between her teeth for a few minutes, thinking about it, staring red-eyed at him and then the papers. She finally said the words, but it took her a while longer before she could think of him as her man. She needed to ask him what it meant, what changes saying those words would bring her.

"When daylight hits tomorrow," she asked, "what will it mean to be your woman?"

"Let's talk about it first thing in the morning," he replied.

When she opened her eyes that morning, she was on the couch, fully clothed, a blanket covering her. He lay in his sleeping bag on the floor beside her. She knew he kept "away gear," as he called it, at all times in his car: a sleeping bag, blanket, and a small duffel holding a fresh change of clothes and other personal belongings. When she looked down at him, he was awake, with his hands resting under his head, staring at her. She wanted to talk right then, but he convinced her to wait until after they had showered and dressed so he could take her out for breakfast.

"It's way past first thing in the morning," she said to him after the waiter seated them at a table with a view of the Pacific ocean at Omar's Seaside Café.

"How come revolutionaries talk like that," she said. "I mean, why do you call me your woman instead of girlfriend?"

"Because, girlfriends come and go, but a woman sticks with her man in bad times and good."

"And what does a man do for his woman?"

"You tell me, Loretha. What do you want from me?"

She wanted to know that he loved her, but through all the talk of belonging to each other that he had introduced, the word love hadn't been uttered. Really, the only time she'd heard him speak of love was in the abstract. He said he loved all black people, and beyond black people, he loved humanity and freedom. He said he loved his brother Rodney, and he loved his grandparents because they raised him. But his kind of love seemed like a duty, like he had a taskmaster marching around in his head, making him say the words.

"Do you love me, Solly?" she asked. "I don't mean because I'm black or because you feel sorry for me, but do you love ... *me*?"

She waited for him to answer and grew a little anxious when he took his time, looking at her for what seemed to be the longest of moments. The drama of the past night had left her tired in a way that gave her the courage to look back at him, steady except for a few blinks, trying to read past his motionless stare to hear the words in his mind. He finally spoke, without smiling.

"Yeah, girl, I love you," he said.

Chapter 8

Loretha discovered that being the woman of a revolutionary was an unpaved road full of rocks to maneuver around and stumble over. Solly gave her a real gold ankh bracelet for her wrist and a solid gold cartouche for her neck but nothing gold for her finger. He gave her restless nights alone for weeks at a time and then acted like he owned her when he returned, questioning her about who she'd been talking to and where she'd been if he should happen to call when she was away from home or work. Sometimes he'd wait until the middle of the night to ask, after he'd spent himself inside her, after he'd coaxed her to respond the way she knew he wanted her to, and again, she'd comply. She'd make him feel like the king of his revolutionary world.

"Called you today, Loretha. Where you been? Why you weren't here?"

Sometimes, though, all she got from him when he'd show up again was wordlessness and pensive, faraway looks. And the nights he lay beside her, she'd soak up his tension as he buried his head in her neck. If she moved or turned, he'd simply tell her, "Don't you go nowhere."

She even wrote Mamie about Solly and Mamie answered:

Girl, some men are strange, and when love hits them they can get crazy, especially when part of them feels they're too big and bad for what they're going through. Seems to me that's your Solly. He's marking his territory and you're it. Just don't let him hit you. If he raises his hand you tell Daddy Henry and Junebug straight off.

Then there was the matter of Solly and other women, and they were the ones who let her know they were around, lurking, taking some of his time away from her and from the revolution.

Late spring 1970. She spent Juneteenth at MLK Park with Solly. The URV called it Freedom Day and hosted a picnic for its members graduating from the state universities and a few of the community colleges around. Loretha sipped lemonade from a plastic cup, and listened to Solly in his jubilant, speech-making mood, while surveying the scenes around the park as he spoke. She let her eyes pan and capture snapshots of the good-looking women there, some with their mortarboard tassels pinned to their sleeves. She spotted Marcus leaning sideways with one arm stretched out toward his latest girlfriend as he slowly backed her against a tree and pressed his nose against hers, all the while grinning, and she looking as though she just loved the attention. Then they danced away from the tree, holding onto each other really tight, even though the music was fast and others around them gyrated and swayed quickly, some even danced without partners. Suddenly, the music stopped on Solly's command.

"Black power!" he said, his legs spread-eagle, arms raised above his head, fists clenched, like he was ready to pounce or charge forward, or both.

"Let's pour a libation," he said, "to all those black folks in Texas slaving on for two whole years after freedom came because Mr. Charlie wouldn't tell them they could leave the plantation."

"Amen!"

"They didn't know when freedom came, so they made up a date, Juneteenth."

"Teach, brother!"

"Now that's genius and we have to be like them. This here paper we just got don't make us free, you know. It's what we do that counts. Party hard while we can, ya'll, because the struggle is just beginning."

Shouts of "Rap on!" and "Right on!" and "Tell it like it is!" came from the crowd. When the speech-making ended, the poets took over. When they finished, the music started again, and at each table someone had a battery-operated portable record player blasting Gil Scott-Heron, Curtis Mayfield, or the Last Poets. Solly worked the crowd, high-fiving, and revolutionary handshaking with the men, hugging and kissing the women, telling them how good they looked before finally dancing and working his way back to Loretha's table.

"You feeling all right, baby?" he said. She was about to answer, but he took a bite of her chicken and danced back out into the crowd, singing with his mouth full. "Be back in a minute, baby," he said. "Black is beautiful, ya'll!" he said, chewing and laughing at the same time.

Black is beautiful, she echoed in her thoughts. She was happy for Solly, glad about his accomplishment, and glad he was popular and that people listened to him. In a way it was her celebration too, because everybody—women and men—knew her as Loretha, Solly's woman. And at times, someone would stop by her table to talk and make her feel good about her link with him and her place at the picnic.

"Hey Loretha, you looking good today, girl. Solly treating you right?"

But when the sun started going down, signaling the end of the picnic, and talk began about who was having a party and where, Loretha found herself riding in Solly's car back to her apartment. She didn't get an invitation to dress up for a night out. Instead, she reluctantly accepted his peck on her cheek, realizing he had aimed for her lips but she moved away. And when he told her to get a good night's rest and he'd talk to her in the morning, she said nothing. She spent her evening reading and wondering which of the females she'd seen that day would be his woman that night.

She knew that those other women wondered what he saw in her by the stares she'd get from them when they observed her working in the Village or at the bookshop. She wondered too, but not about what he saw. She just figured she had something he needed all those other women didn't have. She thought about Mamie's advice and wondered how long it would last, her identity as his revolutionary woman, and if she ever felt the urge to break free, what her life would be like without him.

For Loretha, ordinary existence inched on, day to day, season to season, year to year, but in the vortex of time between 1970 and 1973, life handed her a string of troubles that tore deep into her spirit. And each time trouble taunted her, her revolutionary lover showed up so she could lean on him. She couldn't quite figure out how he knew bits and pieces of what the trouble was. She was just glad the invisible currents of thought, urban grapevines snaking through the streets of the city, worked as well as they did.

The day Solly brought news to her about Junebug, she had bolted awake that morning to the sound of loud popping noises. It took her only a couple of minutes to realize the sound came from kids playing with firecrackers left over from the Fourth of July. It had happened before, but this time, getting up and going about her routine didn't make the sound go away. Only the children's laughter left her head; the popping noise, like quick gunshots, remained, following her to work and lurking beneath the surface of her awareness as she went about her duties.

At work, she thought she heard Solly speaking to Professor Howard in the back of the bookshop and figured he must have come in through the Village entrance. But then they both came up front. Professor Howard wore her Earth Momma face, and Solly looked half stern with his mouth turned down in a frown and half pitiful with his eyes fixed in a pleading stare.

Loretha knew something awful had happened when Professor Howard wrapped her long arms around her and then handed her over to Solly as if whatever it was that brought them would crack her open if they didn't hold on tight. Loretha tried to speak, but Solly pressed his fingers over her lips and guided her into the library, still holding her close as he told her the news.

Junebug had been shot dead driving down the street in his delivery truck. He got caught in the crossfire between rival street gangs shooting it out in the noonday sun like twisted cowboys in a bad western movie. She stared at Solly in disbelief, then pulled away from him, instinctively hitting at her chest to make the pain ripping through it go away. She heard him say he'd drive her out to the house to be with her folks, and she strained to hear him through the disbelief and grief rising in her all at once.

The revolution went on hold, for Loretha's man stayed with her and her folks the rest of that day and night. And during that brief time, she felt sure of his love with all its imperfections and possessiveness. While Loretha comforted her parents, Solly answered the door for neighbors and people from Fannie's church coming by, bringing food and condolence cards with dollar bills folded inside. When she saw that Henry couldn't take any more grief without his bottle of Scotch and his Mason jar, she nodded for Solly to watch over him, and he did, taking Henry—Brother Emmitt, Solly called him—out to the shed where he could grieve and cry in private.

Because of the way Junebug died, his funeral was a long procession of speeches filled with indignation and remorse about the growing gang violence threatening to destroy Desert Haven. When it came time for Reverend Gilliam to deliver the sermon, Loretha thought he sounded so mad and hurt that he threw away all pretenses of speaking proper English, and pulled his island patois up from his roots, spitting out words to the heavens.

"That weren't no hunting rifle what killed our young brother Henry Isaiah Emmitt Jr. and what's cutting off the lives of so many of our young peoples," he said. "Those were guns invented just for killing people, and you all know like the good Lord knows it's sure a sin. We don't own no gun-making businesses," he said. "Ain't no factories what makes guns nowhere near Desert Haven. We don't drive the trucks delivering them guns, but somebody sure knows how to get them into our streets and into the hands of our young folks, and people I tells you, that's got to stop."

When it was over, Solly told Loretha about how his grandparents had changed and picked up the pace toward their own deaths after his brother Rodney died. He told her she ought to watch over her folks more because they might do the same. She went with him to put flowers on Rodney's grave and on his mother's too. Then she walked with him a few yards more to the graves of his grandparents, and he sat on the ground and cried.

She cried with him.

On a Sunday morning in the winter of 1971, six months after Junebug died, six months after Solly warned Loretha to watch her parents because the death of the young can be hard on the old, Loretha arrived at her folks' home. She quickly closed the door, blocking the warm, desert Santa Ana winds from blowing leaves and dust in behind her.

"I'm sure glad you could come home today," Fannie said.

"It's Sunday, Mom. I always come on Sunday."

"It's lonesome up in here," Fannie said. "I miss the noise with Junebug gone."

Loretha's eyes searched her mother's face and body, looking for signs the time had come to sound an alarm, to call a doctor or the healing matrons of her mother's church.

She went to her folks' home more often now since Junebug's death. Most Wednesdays when Solly was around, he'd drive her there after work, and on Sunday she'd take an early morning bus. Each time she came, Fannie would tell her something about Junebug that she missed. Fannie stayed at home a lot more during the past six months, and sometimes she had to be coaxed out the house.

"You feel like going to church today, Mom?" Loretha said.

Only seconds after she voiced the question, her eyes found the sign she feared. Fannie had her shoes on wrong, with a different-colored shoe on each foot.

"I'm ready to go, Loretha. Can't you see I'm all dressed … just waiting on your daddy to come out that shed and crank up the car?"

Loretha limped and then caught her stride, moving quickly toward Fannie, perceiving another sign more frightening than the first. Fannie's mouth had started moving slowly, and her words were slurred. She reached her mother just in time to break her fall and keep her head from banging against the floor.

"Hold on, Mom," Loretha said. "I'll get Daddy, you hang on now, hear?" When she saw Fannie's intense, conscious stare, she took it as assurance that her mother had the will to challenge what was happening to her. Loretha gently laid Fannie's head down and marshaled her own will to move her body as fast as it could go. She reached the back door, banged it open and yelled for Henry to come quick because her mother had fallen. Her show of physical agility didn't end there, for when Henry bent down to pick Fannie up and carry her to the car, Loretha bent too and helped him lift her. Then she limped quickly again to bang open the back door once more, clearing the way for Henry, grabbing Fannie's TV blanket from the couch on her way out.

They laid Fannie on the back seat of Henry's long, old Cadillac and covered her with the blanket. Loretha managed to squeeze onto the floor behind the front passenger seat so she could hold her mother's head and talk to her while Henry sped up to the General. By the time they arrived, Fannie was unconscious.

"Mrs. Emmitt had an acute cerebrovascular accident," the young emergency room doctor told Loretha and Henry, after they had been waiting for someone to talk with them for a long three hours.

"A what?" Henry shouted at the doctor. He hadn't had a chance to settle into his Sunday drinking before Fannie collapsed, so he was sober, agitated, and afraid, and Loretha tried to calm him.

"A stroke, Daddy," she said. "Mom had a stroke."

"Well, why couldn't he just say that?" Henry said.

"Where is she now? Can we see her?" Loretha said.

"I want ... my wife."

"Daddy, please, let's listen to what the doctor has to say."

The young doctor said Fannie would be moved to the acute ward as soon as a bed became available. She was still unconscious, and more tests would be conducted over the next few hours in order to determine the extent of the damage to her brain and other internal organs.

"What else you got to tell us? Is she gone live?" Henry said.

"We can't give you a prognosis just yet. We're still running tests," the doctor said, appearing unperturbed by Henry's impatience.

"When can we see her?" Loretha asked quietly, knowing with certainty that they needed to be near Fannie, just as she needed to know they were around to comfort her even though she couldn't respond.

"We have to ask you to continue waiting here. The medical team is still working to stanch the hemorrhaging in her brain. You'll be able to see her once she's been stabilized."

They waited hours more, Loretha and Henry, moving back and forth from the plastic chairs to the wooden benches in the emergency room at the General. The daylight hours of Sunday stretched into the night and on into Monday. They prayed and looked anxiously down the halls for the young doctor to come tell them they could see Fannie. Henry told Loretha he knew it was a shame, but he sure wished he had his bottle of scotch with him. She told him she understood. What she didn't say was what she figured they were both thinking—that the doctor would return and tell them Fannie was dead, and neither was ready to hear that.

"I already miss her, 'Retha. Even if she survives this, what'd that doctor call it? Some kind of accident, that's what he said. She won't be herself no more. You know why this happened, don't you? She's pining away for Junebug." He was sitting on the bench now, leaning forward, holding his head, aiming his eyes toward the floor.

Loretha listened to his every word. While she held on firmly to the crisis gripping her mother, some of her attention turned to Henry as his sadness started to sink into her.

"I miss him too, you know," her father said. "Least Fannie could tell the world how much she misses him." He looked at Loretha. "You believe me, 'Retha?"

"I believe you, Daddy. Why don't you sit back and rest while we wait?"

"When he was alive, I couldn't tell him how much I loved him, and now that he's dead, I can't tell nobody how much I miss him. I let him down."

"You did your best. Can't nobody do no better than that," Loretha said.

On Monday afternoon, Fannie was moved to a bed in the acute ward, and the matrons in white from her church started filing in to keep watch over her. A short matron with a high-pitched voice took charge and insisted that Loretha and Henry go home, get some sleep, eat, and freshen up. She told them someone would pick them up later that evening to bring them back to the hospital.

That year was hard for the Emmitt family. By the end of it, Fannie had regained consciousness but was paralyzed and couldn't walk. One side of her face was paralyzed too, and she had trouble speaking. Henry retired from his job at the tire plant and started drawing his pension so he could be with her. He put their house up for sale, and he planned to use the profit to move to an apartment in a low-income housing complex for seniors, owned and operated by the biggest Baptist church in Desert Haven. Desert Paradise the complex was called, with nurses on staff, a physical therapy room, and a Twelve-Step Program, because a lot of elders there were alcoholics like Henry.

Loretha spent her weekends helping the church matrons take care of her mother and helping her father clean the house and get it presentable for showing to prospective buyers. Solly pitched in, helping to paint and using his skills to do electrical repairs. The year slipped into the next with Loretha grateful that her folks had a lot of life in them still, and she saw the way they clung to each other in the wake of their troubles as the deepest kind of love.

In that same vortex of time, Loretha witnessed Professor Howard being brought to her knees by Marcus. He disappeared, and nobody, not even Solly, claimed to know his whereabouts. Loretha knew Marcus was the sun, moon, and stars of the professor's life, and she wondered if this blow would take the older woman down just as losing Rodney had taken out Solly's folks and losing Junebug threatened to take out hers. When this thought rippled through her mind and she brought it to life in her journal, she decided then she'd do all she could to help the professor. As the days turned to weeks without Marcus, Loretha watched as the professor brooded, alternately sitting for hours staring out the window of the library, then moving like a whirlwind through the bookshop and Freedom Village, cleaning up, rearranging, decorating, washing, painting, dusting. It was in the midst of one of these frenzies that Loretha took a chance and pulled a move from Solly's playbook. She walked up to the professor from behind, wrapped her arms around her, laid her head between the older woman's shoulders, and begged her to stop.

"Dear Professor," she said. "Please quit. Let's just close the shop for a while and go sit in the library so we can talk and cry about Marcus."

When she felt the professor's stomach heaving in and out, she realized Earth Momma had emerged and was already crying.

Loretha remained with the professor that evening, looking through photo albums of Marcus in his boyhood, listening to her talk about how sweet and gentle he could be, hearing how she worried he wouldn't be able to hold his own around rougher kids. Then came the time that he got into his first fight and was suspended from school, and she discovered that he had beaten the other kid pretty bad. Then she told Loretha what she feared: that a side of Marcus she thought he'd grown out of had come back to live with him.

"I know," she said, without Loretha uttering a word. "A lot of youngsters close up and stop talking when they reach their teens. But Marcus was different. The look in his eyes. An awful, empty look."

"Empty?" Loretha questioned.

"Yes. So empty it scared me. It was like his mind wasn't with his body, like something had captured it, and left that empty look in its place. My papa saw it too, and said the evil eye caught Marcus, but you know I wasn't going to believe anything like that. Not my son."

Loretha was surprised when she heard the professor talk that way about her own son, as if he were possessed. *Damn crazy fool* is what Solly would have called him, but Loretha preferred to think of Marcus as troubled, disturbed, out of balance.

The professor told Loretha the school counselor had said not to worry. Marcus was probably just using her as target practice for his fearless, manly look. Boys do things like that. It's one of the ways they try to protect themselves, mostly from each other. She told Loretha whatever gripped him seemed to pass when he started high school, and he made it through to college just fine, even ran track until those painful muscle cramps started. That's what kept him out of the military.

"Did I ever tell you Marcus was best friends with Solly's brother when they were growing up? Yes they were. Before Solly left for the army, he would watch out for both of them. Sure is a shame about Rodney."

Then she said how she was amazed Marcus got those folks to safety the night of the fires without both his legs swelling after all that running and jumping.

"And girls, they like him, you know," she said. "I'm glad he's holding out for the right one before he settles down."

"Professor Howard, I want to tell you something. I hope you won't get mad."

Loretha waited for a sign that she could step further into the expanding room of their relationship, but the professor just kept turning pages of the photo albums, calling Marcus's name, almost wailing about his disappearance, and wondering why nobody could tell her where he'd gone.

When the professor finally became silent for more than a minute, Loretha decided to speak up again. "Earth Momma," she said.

"Yes, Loretha," the professor said, lifting her head slightly and glancing at Loretha over her glasses. That very moment, Loretha imagined her own mother next to Professor Howard. Fannie had worried about Junebug so much and prayed so hard he'd turn his life around that her body shook.

"Take care of yourself," Loretha said. "Love yourself."

Then she placed pillows behind the professor's back and searched the room for her reading blanket. Finding it, she spread it over the professor's lap, all the while aware that the professor's eyes, Earth Momma's eyes, followed her around the room.

She left to make a pot of tea, and when she returned to the library, the professor had dozed off, but her nap was fitful. Loretha watched her for a while longer, guarding her mentor, and she wrote her a note, telling her something she knew her mother would say. She just had to have faith that Marcus was okay wherever he'd gone, and when the time came, he'd get in touch with her.

"After all," Loretha wrote, "Marcus loves you as much as you love him."

When Solly called the bookshop looking for her, Loretha told him she was spending the night with the professor. She asked him to pick up her medicine and bring it to her, and he told her he would.

Chapter 9

The day would come when Loretha would step out of her cave and stand up to Solly. She didn't plan to, though. The situation forced her. Preserving herself became more important than pleasing him.

Yet when the urge to test how her tomorrows would be without him finally came, it hit hard. It came in the spring of 1973, after he disappeared again. This time he stayed away for more than a month. When he suddenly reappeared, he said he had gone to Arizona, and he tried to step back into her life as if nothing was different or as if the difference had no meaning she should care about.

"I had to meet some friends in trouble," he told her. She glared at him, trying to stare him down. When she finally released her voice, she breathed and spoke hard and fast.

"Friends? What friends? You've never talked about friends in Arizona. Couldn't you call? What's your friend's name? Who is she?"

He counted money, lots of it, as she spoke. She waited and watched, handling her anger with silence, wondering what he'd say next. When he raised his head, she saw a look that said he was checking things and still trying to figure how to approach her. She kept glaring, unwilling to relinquish any ground or accept his explanation, and finally unwilling to be compliant.

"It's the truth, Loretha," he said, "I need you to trust me, just hang with me, girl, okay?"

He put the cash on the table and took a gun from a holster snapped to his belt and laid it there too. Then he turned his back and walked, head down, toward the window. She had figured he had a gun, but this was the first time he exposed her to it. She looked unthinkingly at the evidence of trouble her man placed on her table, waiting for her anger to turn to fright. When it didn't, she spoke again.

"The gun, Solly; am I supposed to trust the gun too? And the money?"

As Solly turned toward her, she saw on his face what she read as surprise, which he tried to mask, having turned to look at her too quickly. Her mistrust was hard at work now, feeding possibilities to her. Perhaps his surprised look was part of his story, part of his game to convince her. Perhaps he was playing with her.

"I'll put them away if it makes you feel better."

He moved slowly, stuffing the money into an inside pocket of his duffel bag. He removed the holster from his waist, slipped the gun back into it, and placed them in the duffel too.

"There," he said. "Loretha, I need to stay here with you for a while. Not long, just long enough to get my head back together." Then he asked her again to trust him.

"No, Solly, no," was her answer, her voice coming from a part of herself so recessed she was hearing it for the first time. "You're playing with me, and it's not working this time."

She stood rooted in place, looking at him as he moved slowly toward her. He reached for her, and she heard him forcing words out in a whisper. It was a muffled plea, revealing, yet not revealing.

"This ain't no play, Loretha." His hand gripped her arm tightly and pulled her to him. She leaned into his grip, clutched his shirt, and dug her nails into his skin.

"Then tell me, Solly, what it is, so we can both know."

"You don't need to know. If anything happens to me … more trouble, you won't be in the middle of it. I'm asking you again, Loretha, can you handle it? Can we trust each other like this?"

She pulled at him for hours with words and questions, searching for the secret she couldn't unearth as their bodies fused together. For once, she felt in control, powerful and strong, and the feeling was too precious to give up. Still filled with anger and mistrust hours later, they lay tired, yet unmoved.

"Look, I promise," he said. "I won't ever do you like this again. I don't want to now. Why won't you believe me?"

"I told you my secrets, Solly. "Trusted you with them. Nobody knows but you."

"That's different," he said. "You haven't told anybody else because you're ashamed. You don't accept that part of yourself yet."

"Oh, so you think this is different? You're ashamed too or else you'd speak up. It's just not right, Solly. Not right. Tell me the truth or you can't stay here."

"Make up with him," Professor Howard told her several days later. "A wad of money and a gun aren't reasons to dump a good man. You know how many preachers hide cash under their bed and keep a loaded shotgun right next to it? They'll shoot you too if you mess with their stash."

"But he won't tell me what's going on," Loretha protested.

"Keep both fires stoked and he will," said the professor.

Meaning? Loretha asked with her look.

"Your fire, letting him know you're not his fool." Pausing, she pushed her glasses up, and then shook her finger as if to punctuate her certainty. "And the fire in him for what you've got."

She's back, Loretha thought, and she smiled at the sight of the professor being her old self, returning in spirit from the grief of losing Marcus.

It was all over the news the next day, front page headlines in the newspaper with an evening edition and special broadcasts on television. Two headless, burned, male bodies were found in the desert along with a cache of money believed stolen during the 1968 southside riots. The report said the bodies were those of black militants, and the FBI was offering a $50,000 reward for information leading to the arrest of three armed and dangerous fugitives. Loretha's heart jumped with relief when Solly and Marcus weren't mentioned; neither were their mug shots shown among those flashed all over the papers and television.

She knew it had to be Solly when she heard the knock on her door that night. His duffel hung from his shoulder by a single frayed strap, and he held a brown paper bag with a solitary red rose and a bottle of ginger ale in it for her and wine for himself. She didn't ask where he'd been the last few nights. She was so glad to see him after what she heard on the news that she simply reached out and pulled him in. She didn't resist when he thrust his face at hers groping for a kiss.

She cooked dinner and he watched. He set the table and she watched. They ate in silence mostly. Finally, she spoke.

"What made you stop by?" she asked as she glanced at the duffel standing closed and upright by the door.

"Professor Howard said you wanted to see me."

"She knew where you were?"

"No, I called the Village after I heard the news. I didn't want her to think Marcus was dead out there in the desert or on the run from the FBI."

"Where is he?"

"Your guess is as good as mine," he said. "Hope the brother is getting himself back together."

"Then how do you know he wasn't burned up in the desert?"

"I don't know," he whispered. "But I don't want Professor Howard to think he was. It might kill her."

"So what did you tell her?"

"I lied. Told her some guys I know think they spotted him up near Canada."

She reached to pour more wine into his glass, but he took the bottle and began drinking straight from it. She watched him swallow what must have been a glass full in one gulp, place the bottle on the table, suck his teeth, and blow air from his mouth like it was smoke. She glanced again at the duffel still propped by the door. A picture of Solly and Marcus together, riding north up the highway toward Canada, formed in her mind. But the vision quickly and mysteriously changed and they were riding through a desert and then down a narrow road shaded by tall tropical trees. She wondered how long it would be until she finally learned the truth. Solly turned his face toward her and took her hand.

"It's bad out there, Loretha," he said. "Brothers are losing their minds. Correction. Something has invaded our heads and we are losing our minds."

"You are including yourself," she said. "Why?"

"Revolutionaries killing each other, fighting over women, money, and power they don't have, and I'm watching it all go down. Instead of hanging together, we're tearing ourselves up, destroying everything we fought for."

She eased her hand from his, noting how he let her, how his hand became limp. She picked his up and held it, stroking it as he spoke again.

"Revolution ain't possible," he said, "unless we figure out how to trust, unless we take a chance on each other. I've read Malcolm, Martin, Fanon, and a whole bunch of others, looking for some answers, and I ain't no closer to knowing how to get us to unite than Marcus, and he's somewhere on the run, maybe."

"Patience, Solly. Didn't Malcolm say patience creates unity? You ought to be patient with yourself. Maybe then you'll come to see what unity means for you, and us."

She learned that the money he had with him the night they struggled and fought was the remains of the Brotherhood's stash, and the few loyal members left holding on wanted it to go to Professor

Howard. At least, he told her, it would do some good at the Village.

The next day they started looking for an apartment, big enough for them to live in together.

A month later, on a weekday morning, a police car pulled in front of Solly's car and forced it to the curb. Loretha looked at him, and his eyes narrowed as he quickly surveyed the scene. Three police cars and six officers, all springing swiftly from their vehicles and drawing their guns at the same time.

"This ain't no traffic stop, Loretha. This many cops means I'm going to jail. They're gonna open your door in a minute. Get out with your hands up, but not before they tell you to. If they take you downtown too, don't be scared. They ain't got nothing on you. Be strong, baby."

They'd moved into a two-bedroom duplex only three miles south of New Haven Street. Five minutes more and she'd have been at work with Professor Howard, and Solly would have gone about his business, hustling again and trying to figure out which way the revolution was headed and what his place in it would become.

Instead, she heard a policeman yelling for her to get out of the car with her hands up, and she did as she was told. She noticed people watching. Window curtains parted. Second-floor windows opened, and she saw people's faces framed in them. An elderly man taking an early morning walk from the corner store stopped. He placed his bag of goods on the sidewalk and folded his arms across his chest. Soon others joined the old man, and a small crowd gathered.

She looked toward Solly. He was leaning against a squad car with his arms spread out as if he were going to gather the metal hood and squeeze it, when she felt herself being pushed against the hood of the squad car blocking Solly's from the rear. She could no longer see him, but she heard him shouting for her not to be afraid and a policeman telling him to shut up.

Strange hands searched her and made her empty her purse and pockets, and the same hands pushed her into the squad car. She knew Solly had been pushed into another. A metal grid separated the front seat of the car from the rear, with Loretha in the back, alone, already locked up.

The car sped off, and she looked around at the familiar shops, buildings, and people she was leaving behind to enter another world. The speeding car with its screaming siren rushed her to police headquarters. She knew from hearing Solly deal with jailed revolutionaries and everyday people appealing to the Brotherhood with complaints about police mistreatment, that she was entitled to one phone call. The only person she could call was the professor, but she wondered when she'd be allowed to, and if she'd be let go in time to take her medicine.

"Where's Marcus Howard?"

She was sitting in a room furnished with a badly scratched table and four chairs positioned around it. She had been taken from the police car and led directly there, bypassing people lined up to be fingerprinted and booked. She looked around for Solly but didn't see him, and she wondered if he were present, looking at her, unseen.

A lone light fixture hung over the table in the room. It held a bulb so bright the heat from it made Loretha sweat. She thought the black detective sitting across from her looked menacing, but she'd seen the look before on the faces of revolutionaries appearing hard and uncompromising about the point they wanted to get across. *Same mask, different purpose,* she thought, looking from one detective to the other and trying not to let fear overtake her.

"I don't know where Marcus is."

"Are you nervous?" Then without waiting for her to answer they asked her why she was nervous. Loretha didn't bother to respond, but she kept frowning, as if a furrowed brow would help keep her mind empty of thoughts except those about her own survival.

"Where were you on the night of April fourth, nineteen sixty-eight?"

Loretha squinted because of the bright light shining down on her, and moved her mouth without speaking for a few seconds. That question, like the first, surprised her, and she told the two detectives that she left work and went home and stayed there until morning.

"Are you lying?"

She told them she wasn't, and they asked her what took her so long to answer the question.

"I had to think," she said. "It surprised me, I didn't expect it."

"Don't think, just answer the question. Where were you on the night of April fourth, nineteen sixty-eight?"

"I told you, I left work and went straight to my apartment."

"Were you with your hoodlum boyfriend robbing the Desert Haven First National Bank on the night of April fourth, nineteen sixty-eight?"

"What? No," Loretha said. Then she closed her eyes, cupped her hands over her cheeks and began to speak loudly, over and over, as if repeating a mantra.

"I want my phone call. I am not afraid. I want my phone call."

Her interrogators, unrelenting, continued their drill. "Where was your boyfriend on the night of April fourth, nineteen sixty-eight?"

"He was minding his own business. I want my phone call. I am not afraid."

They kept right on questioning her, at times shouting, at others cajoling, and then threatening. Finally, exhausted and shaking, Loretha stopped responding altogether.

"If you don't tell all you know about the robbery, we'll hold you as an accessory to a crime. Do you want to spend five to ten years of your life in jail, Loretha?"

She summoned her voice to make one more declaration. "I didn't do anything wrong and I don't know who did. I want my phone call." Then she vomited.

A female officer led Loretha to the women's washroom to clean herself up. Afterward, she was taken to a holding cell, where there were so many women filling all the bench space she had to either stand or sit on the cement floor. She ended up doing a little of both.

She recognized a few of the other women who had also been detained in the police sweep of Desert Haven. But there were some who claimed to be in the movement that she'd never seen before. She exchanged glances with those she knew, and one warned her not to talk with strangers. They huddled together, and when a woman she'd never seen before introduced herself and tried to get familiar, asking questions and talking about lawyers, she just sat quietly, staring at the floor.

What if this had been a white neighborhood? She asked herself. Would they put this many people in jail? The police had been arresting people that whole week, enough to keep the NAACP and the ACLU busy for months. Half the people arrested claimed their rights weren't read to them, including Loretha, but no charges were filed against her. By that evening, she was free to go home. She started shaking again when she found Professor Howard waiting outside for her.

"You know how news spreads in Desert Haven," she told Loretha. "Not long after you and Solly were picked up, I got phone calls and visits from people describing the whole scene to me."

"What do you think is going to happen next?" Loretha asked.

"That's hard to say, but I've already spoken with Roy about representing Solly."

The professor explained how the police really didn't have any reason to charge Loretha. What they wanted was to pick her brain, find out what information Solly shared with her.

"They kept asking me about that bank robbery," she told the professor. "And they asked me about Marcus. Solly hasn't told me anything about what he did back then, and he said he doesn't know where Marcus is now."

"Well, it's possible Solly doesn't know where Marcus is, but I bet he knows why he left. I don't know what to think, Loretha. I just hope with everything in me that neither of them is mixed up with that robbery."

Loretha nodded, shaking almost uncontrollably as the professor placed her arm around her shoulders and began walking her toward the car.

"You shouldn't go back to that apartment alone tonight, Loretha. Let's pick up a few of your things, and you can stay with me while we find out what's going to happen to Solly."

She nodded again. Yes, Earth Momma, she thought.

At Solly's arraignment, Loretha saw armed police lead him into the courtroom with his ankles shackled and his wrists cuffed. But his head was not bowed, and she followed his gaze as he looked around the room and finally at her. They stared at each other until the bailiff called the court to order as the judge entered.

"The charges are first degree murder and armed robbery, how do you plead?" asked the judge.

"Not guilty," Solly said.

What followed next, as Loretha stared at the backs of the prosecuting attorney and of the defense lawyer, was a war of words and will. The prosecutor argued that Solly was so dangerous he shouldn't be allowed bail. And the defense countered, arguing that before now Solly had never been arrested on felony charges. The prosecutor replied that she had evidence placing Solly at the scene of the robbery and the murder of the bank guard. She stated that the murder weapon was found in the desert along with some of the stolen money and two decapitated bodies burned beyond recognition. When she said that, Roy Adams, the defense attorney, revealed information that caused people in the courtroom to gasp.

"Your Honor, the prosecutor is hiding something here. That gun was issued to a police officer and never reported missing. What's more, the officer himself, one Lee Otis Witherspoon, hasn't been seen in weeks."

The prosecutor swung her head to look at Roy. Loretha could see that she was flushed with surprise and frustration, and the judge had to call the court to order again. Loretha turned to watch reporters leaving to get this latest bit of drama out to the public. The judge set bail, and a few days later, Solly was back out on the street.

"You know, baby, the vines work in jail just like they do in the hood. I heard how you shut down on them. You're more revolutionary than you think."

"But I was scared," she said.

"I know you were," he said, holding her close. "But you were brave anyhow. You didn't cave in, and that's what counts."

Seeing so many people she recognized in jail helped her to understand something he told her about how oppression works. The police entered the black community not to protect and serve but to put down and instill fear. She learned later that the police picked up as many black males between fifteen and fifty as they could find, and anybody with them at the time was held too.

"They treat us like we all look alike, but they know the difference. When something goes down that threatens them, they punish everybody, figuring someone will get scared enough to snitch. That bank robbery had gone unsolved too long."

"So Spoon is a cop? He said he was a graduate student down at San Diego State. If he's undercover, how did Roy find out?"

"Roy's got his own street connections, Loretha, and he knows how to work them. Snitches can't be trusted. They turn on us and cross each other too. Give them enough money, some dope, or threaten to kick their asses, and they'll tell all they know."

Chapter 10

Sometimes when trouble wants to pay you a visit, it stops by a friend's house first.

Abruptly, without warning, Loretha didn't see Norah anymore at the General. They'd never allow more than three appointments to pass without spending time together while waiting for Norah's mother. But two months had gone by. Four appointments and no sign of Norah. Loretha asked Julie about it, and when she saw Julie's surprised expression, she thought she must have sounded alarmed or irritated.

"Oh, didn't Norah tell you? She comes on a different day now because her mother's car literally died. Can't be fixed. They have to come when they can drive her father's car. It's an old clunker too. God, I hope that one doesn't give out."

Loretha wanted to believe Julie, but she couldn't quite. Why hadn't Norah told her? Why hadn't she written?

Finally, she received a letter from Norah, short and in someone else's handwriting. It was in the fall of 1973.

I know you've been wondering about me, Loretha. I miss you too. Did you finish reading Dr. Zhivago? How'd you like the ending? Russian novels are always so involved and tragic. Like life, I guess. True. You won't be seeing me anymore at the General. I started hurting again, all over this time, and Dr. Bernard took me off the experimental medicine. I see another doctor every Friday. It was good while it lasted. I really am grateful that at least for a few years my life was almost normal and I could do things for myself. Now I can't even hold my pen to write my own letters.

Loretha wrote back, twice, and said she'd like to ride out to see Norah but didn't get an answer either time.

That same year and season, Loretha's health began a downward turn. At first, she did not consciously acknowledge the changes she began to experience. They occurred slowly, as if they possessed free will and wanted to make their presence known but only in their own good time. So she responded slowly. It was even a while before she'd noticed she'd described fragments of the changes in her medical log.

July 21, 1973: Small spot below breast on left side. Size of pencil erasure. Hurts a little sometimes. Seem to come and go.

August 4, 1973: Spot came back again.

September 21, 1973: Another spot. Below the first one. Both on the left side. Hurts a little sometimes.

The first time she felt pain so sharp that she couldn't ignore it, she was in a deep sleep and it jolted her awake. But the pain wasn't from the inexplicable red spots on her left side. This pain was new. Her thigh muscle knotted up as if gripped by giant claws, and she cried out. Just as suddenly, the muscle relaxed and the pain subsided, but she had never felt pain in her thighs before. Solly turned and held her and asked if she had a bad dream. She said yes, accepting the explanation his question offered, because the pain frightened her, and she still wasn't ready to face its meaning.

Days after the first instance of pain in her thighs, she began noticing a dull ache in her ankles and knees, a dragging ache that grew sharper during the evening and at night. She rationalized that she must be standing too long while at work, and she even wrote that thought in her log. But when the pain in her right thigh returned and lingered, then moved to her left thigh, she could no longer ignore what was happening to her. These were new anomalies, nothing like the arthritic symptoms she felt many years earlier. She didn't know which medicines caused them or if the medicine could be faulted at all. She knew though, that she had to act. She had to finally admit that her body was slipping backward into illness, and the slide worried her. Unless she told someone, she'd be there on that ominous slide alone.

Nine years and eleven months after Loretha Mae Emmitt first met Dr. Claymore E. Bernard, she stuffed her medicines and medical logs into two cloth shopping bags, slung them over her shoulders, and hauled them along with her cane in a cab to the General. She got out across the street from Old Red, at the entrance closest to the research labs. She used her cane when she walked up the slight incline to the door, which opened automatically as she approached.

During the ride across town, she had rehearsed what she'd say. Her health was slipping back into pain and misery, and she really needed to talk with

Dr. Bernard. On her last two visits to the lab, he was nowhere around.

"When is he coming back?" she had asked the lab assistants. "How can I get in touch with him?" She would be persistent this time until she got the answers she wanted to hear. She even rehearsed what to say if they downplayed the changes she was going through, just in case they offered her soothing words in place of information.

Her hunch was only partly right, because that October day, the answers were different.

"Loretha," said Julie, the lab assistant. "Meet Dr. Jenkins. She's taking over for Dr. Bernard for a while."

The new doctor smiled and quickly reached out to shake Loretha's hand.

"Your logs. Let's go over the latest notes," she said.

Loretha cooperated, opening the binder and flipping the pages back to May 21, the date she wrote the first mention of the rash near her breasts. She nodded when Dr. Jenkins said the symptoms were puzzling. But then the doctor said it would be wise to remove her from the study. She promised to work diligently to uncover why the symptoms had returned and why new ones were appearing, and that she would find the right treatment for her under the circumstances.

"But what about Dr. Bernard—what does he think?" Loretha asked, feeling her lips quiver as she spoke.

"Oh, uh, I'm sure he'd agree," Dr. Jenkins said. Then she smiled and spoke softly, bobbing her head at the same time. She told Loretha that she was very familiar with the research, and that everything would be fine during Dr. Bernard's absence.

"I'll let him know your concerns."

"But where is he?"

Dr. Jenkins kept smiling. "Here are two prescriptions, one for pain and the other for swelling. You'll be all right, Loretha," she said.

Loretha left that day with some new medicines, and the General kept the old.

On her next appointment, she tapped with her cane down the back hallway. She arrived at the lab and found it locked. The words, "Laboratory 4 C. E. Bernard, MD, Principal Investigator" had been removed from the glass insert on the door. In their place was a typed notice instructing Dr. Bernard's patients to go to a different clinic. She recognized it as really an old one, back in the main outpatient wing of the hospital. When she'd tapped her way through halls she hadn't walked in years, there was no Dr. Jenkins and no lab assistant. Loretha was back among the waiting sick.

She checked in with the receptionist and sat, all the while looking around at a scene so familiar it was like she had taken a long break, lasting nearly a decade. The waiting room dramas she had forgotten began to play out before her eyes again.

She looked for newness, for something different, for anything that told her that the passage of time had brought change and new meaning. But she saw old sameness. The same soap operas on a wall-mounted television, torn, outdated magazines stacked haphazardly on a coffee table, and a pile of children's toys in a heavy, plastic box shaped like a barrel.

Some of the waiting sick stared at the clock and complained about how long they'd been there. Others slept, like the old man who was slumped and leaning forward. Some watched, like the young man beside him, whispering, seeing to it that his elder didn't slump to the floor.

She finally heard her name called, rose, and tapped her way to see yet another doctor.

He too brought sameness, his eyes familiar. Yes, she'd seen him before, only he was older then. The sight of this new doctor made her dig her fingers into the cane and press it into the floor, hard.

"Morning, I'm Clay Bernard." Then he added, "Junior."

She looked at him and at the chair as if debating what to do, when she heard him invite her to sit, and he touched her arm lightly to help her. She cooperated, not really wanting to, but not knowing what to do next if she didn't.

"I know this must be surprising," he said, positioning his chair so he could face her.

She worked so hard at keeping her composure while he talked, she felt stiff, like her bones locked at the joints and her body grew straps tightening themselves around her against her will. He told her he knew she'd been through a lot lately with her symptoms returning so forcefully. But at least she needn't worry about changing doctors because he'd be there for a while.

"Maybe you ought to see a social worker," he said.

He scribbled a referral and handed it to her. Loretha realized that this young Bernard, with his hair dark brown in all the places his father's had turned gray, was trying his best to comfort her. But the words registered like thuds. Each one, mysterious and foreboding. She wanted the release of tears but couldn't cry. She was wound too tight to break down in front of him.

When Loretha left the General, she walked. She tapped her way past the bus stop and down General Drive, past a pharmacy, a Laundromat, a liquor store, and a delicatessen filled with lunch-time patrons. She walked on past the storefront headquarters of healthcare organizers, and past a new military recruitment outpost enticing young men to enlist because the draft had ended earlier that year.

The tears she had refused to release in young Dr. Bernard's presence could no longer stay dammed up inside, and she cried. She didn't bother wiping them away until a stranger tried to help and gave her a handful of tissues. She thanked the stranger and tapped on, finally stopping at a park, crumpling to the ground under a tree.

Later, she didn't know how long she'd stayed there, crying, wailing, then squinting, swollen eyed at children playing on the jungle gym nearby, but far enough away so that they didn't notice her distress. She wished she had her journal with her so she could write about what was happening to her. When she realized the sun had passed west of the meridian and would soon set, for the days were getting shorter, she pressed her back into the tree and her cane into the ground and forced herself up. She had long since removed her shoes, because her feet had swollen and the leather cut into her skin. She left them under the tree and slowly headed, barefoot, toward Freedom Village.

She periodically rested at bus stops, and she looked around at the people walking, running, talking, and laughing, going about their business. Though she didn't know them, they were her people, because they lived in the same invisible river of existence. They were strong beings in that river, seeming to float in it effortlessly and she envied their vigor. She longed to know them, to be full of life with them, to laugh and flow along, talking and touching, like they were long lost friends.

She moved on toward her destination, walking the last mile of the six separating Freedom Village and the General. With her arms tired from tapping and her body wearied by the stress of joyless walking, she turned off the alarm at the back of the Village and forced herself through the archway to the patio, where she slumped into a corner.

There she wailed and moaned, and the last sound forcing itself from her mouth dragged her down into a cavern so deep she was beyond sleep, beyond dreams, and beyond thought, her body weightless, her essence suspended in the cave deep inside her mind.

She hung there until a sound stirred her, repeating itself like it was trapped in the groove of a damaged record. The sound was familiar, a name. She wondered who the name belonged to, and who was doing the calling. It jolted her and reminded her that she was made of flesh and could feel and see, because she felt pain once again. Even her eyes hurt as the light from above pierced through her lids. Then her thoughts raced up toward the light. She remembered her name, Loretha, and the person calling her, Solly. The record stopped.

"I'm dying," she said.

She opened her eyes and saw them, Solly and Professor Howard. "When you're ready," the professor told her, "I want you to tell us what's going on with you up there at the General."

Chapter 11

It was the middle of winter in 1974, yet the day was warm, almost hot. Bright sun rays beamed through the window of Professor Howard's library, where Loretha sat reading about the history of the General. She was looking at pictures showing its change over the decades, its assumption of power as it sprawled across acres of land, becoming a living, breathing organism able to give or take away life. She propped an envelope containing a note from Mrs. Strom, Norah's mother, against the clay pot of fake orchids standing in the center of the table.

The note said Norah passed away in January, but days before her death she had said that she wanted Loretha to have her books. She also wanted to return the letters Loretha had sent her through the years. They were alike in that way too, for Loretha still had every letter Norah wrote, from the time they met in '64 to the final one sent just before Loretha's brush with the police.

By her calculation, the man Loretha blamed for Norah's death had been missing and unaccountable for his actions for nearly six months. She was certain now the General kept its own secrets. She figured something about Dr.

Bernard's research had always been cloaked, and his disappearance was part of the mystery. She picked up her pen and started writing questions about her own fate, about Norah's, and about the General's research that linked them in ways promising life but delivering death.

She wondered what others knew: Julie, Dr. Jenkins, Dr. Bernard's son. She wondered if they were all in on the secret. She wrote the words "conspiracy" and "cover-up" in big letters underneath her list of questions. The act of writing these words fixed their meaning in her mind as nothing but the absolute truth, and she wanted someone to declare it. She wanted what had happened to Norah and to her to be exposed. But how? She asked herself. What could she do to bring the General's secrets into the light of day, so the whole world would know?

The weather was still warm the next Sunday when Solly drove Loretha to meet Norah's folks. They didn't have to be out to the Stroms' place until noon, but the drive was long, so they set out early. On the way they talked about the road ahead for both of them. Solly said he wanted her to know for sure that he didn't take part in the bank robbery, and he couldn't remember ever telling her in just those terms. She told him it felt good to finally hear him come right out and say it, but she had never asked because deep down her hope had grown so large it had become unshakable faith. When she said this, he pulled off the freeway and drove to a park where they sat in the open.

"You have to understand, baby, if I thought robbing a bank would help our people, I'd rob ten banks in a heartbeat. But this one didn't do nothing but bring trouble down on everybody on the south side. Practically every black man in Desert Haven went to jail. I might still have to take the heat for it, Loretha. The cops want to pin this on me so bad they ain't even looking for nobody else."

"But Roy said the DA doesn't really have a case against you, or anyone for that matter."

"Yeah, that's the problem. You know how Mr. Charlie hates having his game messed with like that. Roy is a good lawyer, but he's fighting inside the same system that's out to get me. There's no guarantee we'll win."

"Do you know who did it?"

"Yeah, I know."

They sat close but not touching, and she sensed he wasn't afraid. The unknown didn't scare him, and neither did the possibility of going to prison. He seemed ready no matter what.

"I hope," she said, "I live to see you through this."

The noise of urban life—cars and trucks rumbling fast down the freeway, the faint chatter and laughter of children playing in the precious winter warmth, the sounds of city nature, birds singing and flying about—all became dreamlike, soothing the fear of the unknown that stirred in her, masking her need for comfort, until he spoke.

"Where's that faith, girl?" he said. "If you can have it for me, you can for yourself too. Remember that big stick you told me about a long time ago? Huh, baby? What better time to show it than now?"

She relaxed completely as he pulled her close. She welcomed the firmness of his arm around her shoulder and the deep way he pressed his fingers into her flesh, gripping hard as if to hold her life inside.

"Tell me something, Solly," she said. "Why didn't you just leave when you found out how sick I am? I mean, you can have any woman you want."

"Maybe I can," he said. "But I'm not your boyfriend, Loretha. I got hip to that the same night I found your medicine. I'm your man. Remember? And a man sticks with his woman in good times and bad."

The Stroms were poor, and Mr. Strom, well into his senior years, worked a second job on the weekends as a clothing store sales clerk. During the week, he taught social studies at Pierce Canyon High School. They were still paying off Norah's medical bills from the time before she joined the research. Mr. Strom had medical benefits through his job as a teacher, but the insurance company wouldn't cover Norah's condition.

Their ranch-style house sat at the base of Pierce Canyon Boulevard before the street snaked up into the hills overlooking a valley. The lawn was brown stubble, and weeds mingled with untended rose bushes. The old yellow station wagon that carried Norah to and from the General sat parked on a patch of bare ground next to the long gravel driveway. Dust and spider webs covered it, and all of its tires were flat. Large cypress and maple trees shaded the house, giving the whole scene a decrepit, gothic look.

Norah's mother greeted her with a wide grin and reached right past Loretha's outstretched hand to hug her.

"My Loretha," she said with a high-pitched laugh. "My Norah's friend. Come in."

Loretha listened to her broken English and imagined that she must have immigrated from some place far away, some place Norah never felt the need to talk about. She wondered why, briefly, until she remembered that she herself never talked about Nettle Creek either when she and Norah were together. All they talked about were books, their favorite characters and writers, and what they were going to do with their lives once cured and no longer in the research project. Norah told Loretha she wanted to become a teacher, and Loretha admitted to Norah that she still held out hope that she could have children someday.

The Stroms' sparsely furnished living room smelled of old rugs. Large cabinets full of books and ceramic figurines lined the walls. A solitary porcelain urn rested on the fireplace mantle just beneath a large photographic portrait of Norah. The portrait had a nature backdrop of a meadow, and a lone turtle dove hovered over Norah's head.

When Loretha introduced Solly, Mrs. Strom shook his hand and held on tight, like she didn't want to let go. When she finally did, they followed her into the dining room and sat at the table where she'd placed a platter of cookies and some cups and saucers. The she left the room to get a pot of tea and offered Solly a glass of red wine.

"Ah, my Loretha, you good? You have cane," she said when she returned.

Loretha and Solly spent the afternoon with Mrs. Strom, listening to her talk about Norah, and Loretha got the impression that Norah's mother didn't have the opportunity to do that very much, especially with someone who knew what her daughter had gone through. She had given birth to two other children before Norah, but each had died shortly after being born. Norah was precious because she lived, despite coming into the world full of ailments. When she made it to her first birthday, the Stroms had a special celebration.

"My Norah bright child," Mrs. Strom said.

"She no do like other kids, you know, she sit all the time. But she do everything in here," she said, pointing to her head.

"She write too and she read good."

Mrs. Strom showed Loretha and Solly pictures of Norah reading stories to a group of children at a preschool where she volunteered just before her health took a downturn again. It was just before she developed a bad sickness, as Mrs. Strom called it, soreness and rashes and pain Norah didn't have before the research. She pointed to the urn on the mantle and said that that was Norah. Someday they would bury her ashes, Mrs. Strom said, but she wasn't ready to let Norah go yet.

"I think the cancer it got her, you know? But they never tell us."

Mr. Strom had tried to talk with Dr. Bernard but couldn't get to see him or get any satisfactory answers about what was happening to their daughter. He even wrote to the hospital. When an answer to his letters finally came, it said that Norah had been reintegrated into regular hospital services, the same thing Loretha was told.

"My husband, he do all the writing for me. He wrote letter to you." She smiled. "I just sign my name."

Then she turned to Solly and told him to get Loretha out of the study while she could still walk and do things for herself and didn't hurt so bad.

"That research no good," she said.

When Loretha told her she'd already been dropped, just like Norah, Mrs. Strom cried.

Nineteen seventy-four was the year Professor Howard's library became Loretha's refuge. She retreated to it after she finished her shift each evening, where she read, wrote, and waited for Solly. Since losing Norah, she'd go there to brood, roll around in grief, and silently but unashamedly pity herself.

In the bookstore and Village, she seemed focused and sharp. But truthfully, staying attentive to her job and the public was hard work. Trying to hide her feelings and get lost in her duties helped her to forget, but only part of the time. So she was glad the professor allowed her to settle in private in the library when nothing was going on.

She appreciated Solly's encouraging her to rely on faith and prayer for strength, yet she read his words as a sign he thought she'd die like Norah did. Solly never prayed, at least never admitted to it, even in dangerous situations. He met force with more force or determined resistance. She interpreted his words as acceptance. He didn't fear death for himself, so why would he fear it for her? He offered her prayer as a blanket to comfort her while she waited for an upturn in her fortunes, or to be thrown out of the game with the hand she'd been dealt.

It was Professor Howard who came to Loretha's rescue, giving her the emotional and mental stimulation she needed, reminding her of that deep, clear stream of pure spirit inside.

"Open your eyes, Loretha. It's daylight, girl," she said.

She asked Loretha if she knew what two things everyone brought into the world, and what same two things they could look back on when it was time to leave.

Over the years, Loretha had gotten used to Professor Howard's asking questions and making statements and not waiting for a response. She was in her Earth Momma persona and kept right on talking, answering her own questions and passing the answers on to Loretha.

"Mind," she said. She told Loretha that her mind could grow beyond any limit set for her or that she set for herself. Her mind could grow beyond arthritis, beyond the research that abused her body, beyond her fears, that her mind could reach the stars and far, far past them.

"The second thing is heart—you know, love."

She said Loretha had a heart that was love itself, whose capillaries and veins didn't stop at the outer reaches of her body. They were attached to the ground and stretched down to the core of the earth. Her task as a human being was to reach that core in mind and spirit with the time she had left, whether one day or a hundred years.

"Come forth by day," the professor said. That's what you've got to do. Use your mind to grow toward infinite wakefulness. Use your heart to grow toward infinite love. That's all there is."

That night Loretha began sewing scraps of multi-colored fabric into a quilted cover for her journal. She gave the journal a name: *Loretha Mae Emmitt's Journey, Coming Forth by Day.*

On her next day off, she showed up at the coalition headquarters for Radical Health Care Reform, a group also operating a free clinic for the homeless and the poor. She planned to find answers to her questions and to expose the General.

The office was located on General Drive, down the hill from the hospital. Most days, protestors congregated, picked up signs and flyers, and went to various places in the city and agitated for free medical care and patients' rights. She had seen them in front of the General when she went for her treatments. She also had seen them at protest rallies in front of City Hall, and she'd courteously take their fliers and newsletters and dutifully read them, all the while wondering about the difference between the treatments she received from the General and what this group advocated. Now their actions had taken on new meaning, and she hoped they'd help with her plan.

She scribbled a note to Solly and placed it on the kitchen table. For the second time in her life, she left home with her medical logs. This time she carried logs for 1973 and 1974 in a black cardboard case. In the taxi on the ride to the coalition's office, she readied herself to release what remained of her own secrets. She was now prepared to tell the world what had happened to her.

"I'm dying," she told the man and woman in charge, Drew and Lottie Frazier, who invited her into a room used for private consultation. "A research project up at the General has cut my life short."

Loretha spent the rest of the afternoon in that room. As she began telling her story, the couple asked if they could record it, and she said yes. They looked at her logs, wrote down the names of medicines, and studied the procedures she followed. They pulled out big pharmaceutical books and pored through them looking for substances with long names they could pronounce but she couldn't. They asked questions.

"Who's the doctor in charge of the research?"

"Was," Loretha replied. "Dr. Claymore E. Bernard. He left back in late September. At first they said he was away on business, then they said he got sick and retired."

"Who took over for him?"

"I saw a lady doctor named Jenkins after that, one time. The lab at the General where I used to see Dr. Bernard and his staff is closed down."

"What was the name of the research project?"

"Name? It was about arthritis. I was born with rheumatoid arthritis. Arthritis Study, I guess."

"When did you become involved in this arthritis study?"

"I signed up in 1964."

"What made you get involved? Were you promised something?"

"To tell you the truth, I thought I was going to be cured. Dr. Bernard said the research was a breakthrough, yes, that's what he called it, a breakthrough."

"Did he ever say you'd be cured?"

"No. But up until last year, it was almost like being cured. He promised me all the free medical care I needed since I didn't have insurance. I got a knee operation, and my friend Norah even got both hips replaced. But things changed back in October. It's almost like the research stopped, like I'd been dropped when Dr. Bernard left.

"What were you told?"

"They didn't explain, just said they needed to find out why the arthritis symptoms came back. But some of my symptoms are new—the skin rashes, and the aching pain in my thighs like something is inside trying to claw its way out."

"What did they tell you about these new symptoms?"

"Nothing yet. They just keep running more tests, and they've changed my medicine twice since then."

"Why do you say you are dying?"

"My friend Norah Strom died last January. She was in the study too. When Norah started getting sick again, they didn't tell her family what was happening to her either."

"Who is your doctor now?"

"Dr. Claymore E. Barnard Jr."

The man and the woman stared at Loretha for a second, mouths open. Then they both said in unison, "His son?"

Loretha spent Monday afternoons at the coalition headquarters for the next month being interviewed and watching as the couple wrote down her story.

When she finished giving them as much information as she had, she kept going there to volunteer her time. She felt hopeful around Lottie and Drew and the others who came into the office and left with a job to do or project to work on. They were sometimes loud, and they laughed a lot, and as they learned about Loretha's story, they'd be indignant over how she was abused. Their zeal spiraled out from them, and she wanted to catch some of it to keep herself buoyed. She didn't bother to ask what she could do to help. She just kept showing up and did whatever looked undone. She made phone calls, created fliers and leaflets, and stuffed envelopes. She even made snacks for picketers, and sometimes when she had the energy, marched the picket lines herself.

The couple asked her to help them gather more stories from people living on the south side about their experiences with health care, health insurance companies, and the General. Loretha told Solly and Professor Howard. The three of them started planning how to stir Desert Haven and surrounding neighborhoods to action.

Professor Howard and Solly talked about using their clout to get local presses to publish stories and articles on health conditions in the community. Loretha, meanwhile, decided to turn her attention to others in the arthritis study. She wanted to know who else had been quietly removed from the study or had died, and who was still alive and able to talk about their experience. So she created a flier with her story on it, asking others in the study to step forward. Professor Howard advertised the flier in the regional independent newspapers.

"My name is Loretha Mae Emmitt," the flier read. Above her name was a picture Solly took of her, standing tall, holding her cane, with both hands resting on its handle. She wore a long African dress with a matching head wrap over her short-cropped hair, and big, round, gold earrings to match the gold cartouche around her neck.

"I was a research subject in an arthritis study at Wilborn Layton General Hospital from January, 1964, until October 1973," the flier continued.

"Around the same time new ailments started showing up in my body, the doctor I'd been seeing for nearly ten years, Claymore E. Bernard, disappeared. No one at the General has told me why my health is failing and what's going to happen to me. If you were involved in this study, have a story like mine or know someone who does, and if you would like to see some action, please get in touch with me."

The flier did its job. She received phone calls and letters from dozens of people who were dropped from the study, and from others who had loved ones or friends who died after being dropped. She wrote and called them back and when she told them she wanted to take their information downtown to the General's monthly public board meeting and demand an investigation, she didn't get any objections.

In the board chambers at the General, Loretha stood behind the lectern and placed a large stack of papers on it when her turn came to talk. She told the board her name and began asking the questions she'd written down while in Professor Howard's library months earlier.

"Where is Dr. Claymore E. Barnard?" she asked. "Why was he allowed to give dangerous drugs to me for almost ten years, to others a whole lot longer, and no one at this hospital stopped him?"

She paused slightly between each question and looked at the powerful men and one lone woman sitting in front of her at a conference table shaped in a semicircle positioned on a raised platform. The lectern where she stood was placed inside the arc of the table, and the people who accompanied her—Solly, Professor Howard, Lottie Frazier, and several others who'd also been dropped from the study—sat in the first row of seats behind her. It seemed to Loretha there was at least twenty feet of space separating her from those who supported her. She thought as she approached the lectern that the room was designed to make ordinary folks with complaints or requests feel small. *It's too late*, she thought. *I don't feel little anymore.*

"These are very serious allegations you are making Miss Emmitt," said the one woman, lowering her head and looking over the rim of her glasses. She was nice looking, younger than anyone else on the board, and she wore a pale blue spring suit that made the dark gray- and black-suited men sitting with her look even older and drab. Loretha thought the woman's act of aiming her stare over the top of her glasses as pretentious, as if she did it to show she had just as much authority and power as the men around her.

"What proof do you have?"

"Proof? Here are written statements from dozens of others about Dr. Bernard's research and what it did to them. I'll be happy to read them." She paused again, held onto the side of the lectern with one hand and waved some of the papers from the stack with the other. "My guess is that someone at this hospital knew all along, so which of you will stand up and do something about it? Which of you will lead the search for Dr. Bernard and make him answer for what he's done?"

Loretha didn't wait for a response. With that question, she turned, secured the stack of papers under one arm, and tapped with her cane back to her seat.

The flier's appearance and Loretha's confrontation with the hospital board made it into the paper the next day, and marked the end of her visits up to the General for treatment. The volunteer doctors at the coalition clinic helped manage her pain while they looked for another physician who would accept her as a regular patient.

"Tell us your story," one of the reporters said. There were two of them from the *Desert Haven Chronicle*. They sat with Loretha, Solly, and Professor Howard around a patio table that had been moved onto the grass so they could sit in the sun.

"When did you first meet Dr. Bernard?"

"November 22, 1963. I remember because it was the same morning Kennedy was shot."

"How long had you been seeing Dr. Bernard before he told you about the study?"

"Well, I wasn't seeing him. I mean, he was new to me. The way doctors rotate around the General, I'd have a new doctor every three or four months. He told me about his research on that first visit."

"Do you remember what he said?"

"It was a long time ago, but I still remember … I mean, I remember how he talked. He asked questions about me, questions like what I wanted from life and what I liked to do. He acted as if he wanted to get to know me. He said I was bright and deserved more out of life than to be stricken with this disease."

"Did he try to get to know you before or after he told you about the research?

"Before, but the nurse had already talked to him, told him I went to Del Rio."

"How did you react to his asking all those questions? Weren't you suspicious?"

"I was nervous, but not suspicious. I didn't know what to expect. It was all so new to me. I told him I wanted to finish up at State but couldn't because of my legs. I told him I wanted to get married and have children someday."

"Why did you tell him that?"

"Because he asked me. 'What do you want from life, Miss Emmitt?' That's what he wanted to know."

"So what did he say about the research?"

"He used the word, 'groundbreaking.' He said it was a new treatment for arthritis and he hinted that it would make my life a lot easier, a lot more normal, and that's what I wanted to hear."

"What did your people, your folks, think of his offer? I mean, didn't you talk it over with someone before signing on?"

Loretha looked at Solly and Professor Howard, searching for clues to the mood behind their expression. She knew she'd be asked questions about her choices and her own complicity in shaping her fate. But when the first of those questions came, she needed extra encouragement, and she hoped she'd see empathy on their faces. They leaned forward in their seats toward her, and so did the reporters, one of whom picked up the microphone and held it in front of her, waiting for a response. But no words reached out to her from Solly and Professor Howard. She couldn't tell what they were thinking. She knew from that moment she'd have to summon strength from within to face the reporters' questions. She turned her eyes away from her companions and stared at the microphone.

"I thought his offer would be my ticket to a new life. My parents would be cautious. I knew that. I didn't want them to get in the way or try to stop me. I never told anybody the whole story until my body started to get sick again. Then I told Solly and Professor Howard."

"You never told your folks anything?"

"Oh yes, I told them about Dr. Bernard and my knee surgery, but I never told them I was part of a research study."

"Why not?"

"Well, like I said, I didn't want them to stop me. But after a while, I realized there was nothing they could do about it, but the secret became part of me, I guess. Something only Norah and I knew. We formed a sisterhood of two. Only her folks were aware of the study because they got her into it."

"Did you ever have misgivings about your decision?"

"Sort of, the year Norah and I met. The protestors hanging around the hospital started to get more numerous and louder, and the press started to pay more attention to things going on there. I just kind of realized one day that I had struck a bargain with Bernard and the General, to give my body over to something I wasn't sure of. Whenever the question would come up in my mind about what I was getting in return, I'd push the thoughts away. I didn't want to face the possibility that I was being used or that I'd made a bet I couldn't win."

"When did you begin to know for sure that something was terribly wrong?"

"In '73. That's when I started to hurt so bad I could no longer deny what I'd known in my heart for over a year, that my body was becoming sicker, with ailments I never had before."

"What made you come forward and complain after you realized your predicament?"

She was silent again, feeling her thoughts as they formed into words and holding on to them before letting them become audible. She swallowed hard, and she suspected those around her could perceive her discomfort as she felt it.

"I just couldn't be silent anymore, because even being quiet started to hurt, if you know what I mean. Yes, I should have questioned Dr. Bernard and the General a lot earlier, but my weakness is no excuse for abuse from the doctor and hospital I put my trust in."

"Why do you suppose none of the others in the study spoke up?"

"My guess is that they'd given up. They placed their trust in a system that deceived them, left them ... us, desperate for any kind of help."

"What do you mean?"

"We were harmed by the very people who were supposed to help us, the hospital and the insurance companies. None of us had health insurance. We were easy marks for somebody like Bernard. God forgive him. It's like being told our lives aren't worth anything. We're in shock and grieving for ourselves."

"It seems you've become their spokesperson," said the reporter asking the most questions. "How does that feel?"

"If that's what I'm called on to do, I think I'm ready and strong enough to speak for them as long as they let me."

Chapter 12

Three years passed.

April 4, 1977, found Loretha wheelchair-bound on a stage at Martin Luther King Jr. Park. Solly guided the chair up the ramp and into a corner shaded by tall palm and oak trees, so she could watch the crowd as it thronged into the park, shouting what the day was all about.

"What do we want? Patients' rights! When do we want it? Now!"

They chanted melodically, rhythmically, one group calling out and clapping hands, and another responding and stomping feet. Loretha tapped her foot to the beat and chanted along with them, softly, saving her voice for the speech she would deliver later.

That day marked a narrowing of the three-year span of time since she stepped from the shadow of her own secrets and exposed Bernard's research. Her body had weakened so much she could no longer stand or walk without help. Yet her mental vitality sharpened from knowing that people listened and found her cause worthy of their concern and action. And she felt Solly changing toward her during those years, monitoring her phone calls and schedule like a godling assigned by a power beyond him that he could neither name nor resist. Their public time together moved Loretha to the forefront, with him driving her to and from speaking engagements and rallies. In private, she crafted the speeches out loud, and he typed them so she could conserve her strength. She learned, with Solly's prompting, to keep her outdoor speeches to fifteen minutes, and she was good at packing a lot of inspiration into them.

"People don't need to hear facts from you," he said. "They want what's in your heart, some of what you've got to help them carry on."

Opposite Loretha on the stage, the musicians set up keyboards, horns, drums, and guitars, and the accidental sounds of the instruments teased the atmosphere and made it jump with anticipation. The sun moved westward as the shadow of the trees spread east across the lawn, cooling the air for the tired yet excited marchers. Like wings of a giant bird in slow flight, the shadow glided across the grass and over Oasis Boulevard, slipping shade to neighborhood kids and old folks sitting in lawn chairs in front of Freedom Village, the bookshop next to it and along the curb. From her place above the scene, Loretha held a clear view of them and the action happening in the park.

The crowd's attention was divided. First they watched the musicians and stagehands do their work to the beat of competing portable radios blaring vintage soul and rock, everything from Marvin Gaye and Aretha Franklin to the Beatles and the Rolling Stones. Then they turned their heads toward the rousing thunder of African, Japanese, and Native American drums playing in succession, at times drowning out the chanters. On the south end of the park near another palm grove providing shade for the food vendors, a Mariachi band played, drawing attention to the scent of peppery hot sausages, and the sweet corn smell of freshly made tamales. The old folks sent the young, fists and pockets filled with money, on a hunt for hot food, sandwiches, soda pop and fruit juice.

Although she led the march from city hall to the park riding in her wheelchair, when it came her time to speak to the crowd, Loretha stood, rising slowly as Solly lifted her forward, led her over to the lectern and held the mike, and she surveyed lines of human bodies still linked by the rhythm of the slogans they marched to all that day.

First, she looked in the direction of her friends, because their familiar smiles anchored and fueled her courage. She reflected as her eyes met theirs that they needed her just as much as she needed them. Each had a private motive to be with her on that day, in that park, heeding the call of that precise social struggle bringing all those people together. Yet they kept their motives out of sight and didn't talk about them. Mine are right out in the open, she thought. But theirs? They think no one is noticing, but I see.

Her vision about her friends had become so keen it was as if she looked beyond them and over the veil dividing dimensions of past, present, and future, through the mist separating the visible from the invisible.

As Solly stood next to her, she imagined another Solly running through the crowd and away, disappearing into a land that looked nothing like the park or Desert Haven.

She nodded at Earth Momma, who waved and grinned, as Roy, standing beside her, aimed the eye of a camera toward the platform. But the scene changed to one living only inside Loretha's head, one that had played out many times over the years, Roy's arm around the professor's waist. This time, the professor smiled up at him and leaned her head against his shoulder. Loretha sensed the presence of someone else near the professor, Marcus, hiding, yet longing to be heard, seen, and touched.

CJ and Dolores stood beside the platform, holding their two-year-old daughter, Malakia. *Dolores is pregnant again,* Loretha thought. A young man stood behind CJ, and his faint image faded in and out as if struggling to form a solid body. Yet his ephemeral, hazy presence couldn't mask how much he resembled CJ.

She was so engrossed in the secrets of her friends' lives, she nearly missed her cue to speak. She let the images disappear when she heard Solly say her name. *My turn, again,* she thought.

"What do we want?" Loretha asked the crowd, speaking into the mike, hearing her own voice echo through the trees, past buildings, and up through the atmosphere toward the clouds.

"Patients' rights!" They responded.

"Thank you all for coming out and walking today for justice and fairness in our hospitals and medical clinics. I don't know about you, but I think when we showed up at the General and City Hall today, the powers that be got the message.

Just a while ago I heard one of the musicians humming as he set up his instrument for the party we're about to have, for the singing and dancing we're about to do in celebration of the victories of our struggle. Now some of you might be thinking we haven't won enough of these skirmishes to celebrate, but, really, we have. We've learned a lot too. We learned when we scored some victories. We learned when we had some setbacks. One of the early lessons we learned is that we have to hang together no matter what else happens, and that's the victory I want us to think about and celebrate today. Just look around at all the people here from all over the region and the state. That's how important this issue is.

People came from all walks of life. Doctors and nurses in their uniforms representing their patients and themselves. Medical student associations are in the park too, and labor unions, here for their workers who can't get health care or pay too much for it.

And there are ministers and teachers among us, and everyday people with no special titles, because they or some member of their family are touched by the issues bringing us together. Stay with me now. I know I started out talking about somebody humming a tune. I'll tell what that tune was in a minute and you'll see why it's so significant.

Nine years ago this month, April 4, 1968, this community almost burned to the ground. We ran from the flames while our businesses and homes were reduced to ashes. During that awful time, the police blocked off the streets as soon as it got dark and wouldn't let anybody out of the area until daylight, and we were under restriction like that for almost a month. People with night jobs had to have a pass from their employer to get back and forth to work. We struggled hard through that time and in the years to follow began building the community back up again. That really marked the beginning of our coming together to bring about change. This very park we are standing in right now is the result of all that hard work and planned change."

Loretha told the crowd that the man after whom the park was named had a message about justice and perseverance and the courage to act, and that the struggle for human dignity included the right to be treated with decency and honesty by a health care system that had been twisted more toward profit than healing. Then she told them that this man's big message was about change, and she broke into a rhyme, a rhythmic whisper, and the crowd got quiet, straining to hear. She was reciting verses of the song, "A Change Is Gonna Come," and somebody started singing it with her and soon the whole park caught the mood and the drums rolled in. The guitars strummed. The horns blew. The people rocked, and Loretha began speaking over the music, her voice sounding loud and strong through the mike.

"Sometimes the winds of change feel like a slight breeze and the change is slow, almost imperceptible. Sometimes they blow hard like those hot Santa Anas blasting out of the desert to the east of us. But we're keeping our stride no matter how slight or how hard the wind blows. We're doing something else too. We're riding the wind, not running, not hiding, but taking it on. As Professor Howard often says, life is always throwing change at us, and if it's not guided, challenged, molded, and met head on, it will overtake us, even if we're the ones introducing it. We really do understand her message. So we deserve to take an evening to celebrate what's been won, keeping our energy stoked like fires for what still lies ahead. Thanks for being change angels, for making sure the change going down in this community, in this city, and in this state is what we want for our greater good. Now let's party, ya'll!"

Night came. Back home, Loretha slept soundly after her day of rolling through the city in her wheelchair, reveling in the park until the sun left the sky and the moon took its place. Pitch blackness descended over her sleeping mind, but with flickers of silver flashing through it like harbor lights, guiding her to a safe and unnamed dream shore.

Part II

∞

September 1977
Puerto de Vida, Mexico
Solly Remembers

Chapter 13

Solly married Loretha and took her on that three-day trip to Puerto de Vida to soothe his own conscience. He was in a world of trouble, and one of the ways he maintained his equilibrium was by occupying himself with things that seemed right. Marrying Loretha and hanging with her were right. Taking her to Mexico for a little fun was right.

When they arrived, it was fully dark, and he welcomed the depth of Puerto de Vida's night. He felt safe inside it, even though darkness usually opened a doorway to danger for him. As a teenager on the streets of Desert Haven, he ran and hid in unlit places from the police. In the military he charged through the portal of darkness to surprise an enemy, or he crouched and waited for one to try surprising him. It was the same when the revolution took over his life, and he slipped in and out of places heavy with blackness, hiding, planning, plotting, and getting over on the society he wanted to remake.

But Puerto de Vida's opaque night had the power to heal, and Solly needed to wallow in it to find himself. After settling in, he sat on the floor of the porch, drinking *cerveza* and watched his driving companion, CJ, walk along the beach. CJ was barely

163

visible, but Solly kept eyeing him anyway until he disappeared from view. Then he turned his head toward the door of the cottage, listening for sounds from his woman inside. He heard only silence.

How Solly found out about Califa was a stroke of luck. True, he watched as some young artists painted her likeness on the walls of Freedom Village, but he was too busy with the revolution to pay much attention then. When his mind became receptive to being wooed by myth, he was at an airport in Southern California, waiting for a flight north. Now when was that? He thought. Then he remembered what the trip was for: to meet with a few revolutionary brothers in the northern wing of the movement. It was in '73, just before all hell broke loose in Desert Haven, and damn near everybody and his daddy went to jail.

He learned about Califa from a travel magazine left behind on a seat in the waiting area. We need a fox like this in the revolution, he thought. He called her the queen, and he was in the right place at the right time to imagine her whispering something sweet in his ear, even if he had the wrong woman by his side at the time.

Actually, it was the woman with him, a background singer for a rhythm-and-blues band, who noticed the magazine first. It had a giant woman on the cover, skin bluish-black, with her nappy hair sticking straight out from her head like oiled spikes. Gold bangles covered her arms from wrists to elbows, and chains hung loosely from her waist, glistening against her skin. She stood with arms crossed over her breast, legs spread wide open, one foot in the water and the other on a piece of land that had the words "Island of California" printed across it in old-style, handwritten letters. *What's your name, queen?* He thought. Then he spotted the word "Califa" printed on the sand, right underneath her foot.

He tried for just an instant to recall the woman's name, the one with him at the airport. He couldn't. But he did remember how he met her, at a concert to raise money for the Southside Brotherhood's Freedom Fund. Gigs like that were always good for picking up women—broads, he'd call them, or foxes. If they earned his respect, he'd call them queens. That's when he was a few pounds leaner and wore his hair thick and bushy.

Solly didn't play around with her for long, the woman whose name he couldn't remember. After that weekend up north, she left to catch up with her band, and he never saw her again.

"That's what I ought to call myself," she told him that day at the airport. "Califa, Soul Queen from California."

He laughed and slipped the magazine into his briefcase.

Indeed, Solly learned that a Spaniard, a novelist back in the 1500s, had dreamed up Califa. He said she was strong like a man and ruled over what pirates and explorers of the day thought was an island in the Pacific Ocean. The island turned out to be the Baja Peninsula, but folks didn't know that back then.

Solly even noticed her in murals of California history at the General. Only he didn't think anything of it, because she didn't look African. As a matter of fact, she didn't even look like a Native American to him.

Maybe that Spanish cat didn't dream her, Solly thought, maybe she put herself in his head like she did mine, and said, "Hey Dude, listen up."

Loretha told him once, back in '76 when her legs had practically stopped working altogether, that she wanted to take a trip, to get away from California.

"Truth is," she said, "I've never been very far from Nettle Creek or Desert Haven. It sure would be nice to visit some place different. Then she added, "Just to say I've done a little traveling. I've been somewhere."

"If you had all the money and time in the world, where would you go?"

"Hmm," she said. "If I had all that, I'd go everywhere and do all the things I can only imagine now."

Then she became quiet, and Solly followed her eyes as they seemed to search around, looking for more to say, a specific place to go in her mind.

"I think I'd start with Mexico though, um, that sure would be nice ... finally ... Mexico."

"We'll have to see about that," he told her. "I'm sure the queen will welcome us to her turf."

But the jaunt to Puerto de Vida was as much for him as for Loretha. He tripped back through their nine years together and finally admitted things didn't go the way he planned. Hell, they didn't even start the way he intended.

It just took time for him to face it. All the while he thought he was in control. "I got this," he said, the night his feeling for her surfaced and shaped itself into words, and he could no longer ignore its presence. "I got this."

He meant it in more ways than one. When he scoped her out in 1968, judged her usefulness and methodically pulled her into his movement and started schooling her in the ways of revolution, he thought he'd give up just a little time. They would have a few dates, and he would show her some loving moves every now and then to keep her in place.

But he discovered that she was holding back, had a side of herself nobody could touch, a solitariness that made her look stuck up. Every now and then, he'd see it and he'd act like it was nothing, as if her reserve added a little flair but wouldn't get in the way of what he needed from her. When he finally realized she had a revolution of her own, he was hooked and he became her foot soldier.

The revolution had already narrowed his vocabulary by the time he first saw Loretha in '68. Depending upon whom he was talking to, every situation had to be spoken of in radical terms, even having a good time. Fun and partying became having a revolutionary good time, and relaxing became laying back and storing up juice for the revolution.

He'd been watching her since that April night after King was killed, and he wondered if he'd live to see daylight. He watched her all that summer. The first real good time he had with her was at the Freedom Village grand opening, in the fall of the same year. That was having a revolutionary good time even though he couldn't say it to her that way. The evening actually felt *wholesome* to him, a word he didn't use often because it wasn't in his militant lexicon. But the evening was all the more enjoyable *because* it was so clean, and people seemed to be waking up from a deep complacent funk, questioning the place history had assigned them to. They were ripe for change, just like Loretha.

Solly was sure he had her figured out right the evening she came to the Brotherhood's rap session, to see what was going on, she told him later, and to ask one simple question.

"What do you mean by the black man is suffering from mental slavery?"

The revolutionary sisters jumped all over her for not already knowing the answer. When she asked another simple question, what about the black woman, they began telling her how she needed to stop straightening her hair and that the next time she came they would show her how to check her whiteness at the door. At that point, he leaped in to rescue her, at least that's what he thought he was doing.

"It means," he said, "too many of us don't know who we are and still happily follow the slave master's program. Glad you came out tonight, sister. It says you're ready to check out some new ways of being black."

Later she thanked him, but he had to note she didn't seem at all embarrassed for having asked the questions or for not knowing the answers.

She was the kind of woman his grandmother wanted him to bring home to meet the family, to marry. Modest and plain, smart and industrious, skilled in the homemaking arts. The kind his folks never saw him with. In truth, he had stopped taking girls to meet his grandparents by the time he left high school. That was before the military, before the forest green and blood-red trails of Southeast

Asia, before Rodney got blown away, and before he became serious about his own life and the revolution.

Loretha was an opportunity. In her, he saw a worker for the movement, a quiet sister-revolutionary, someone nonthreatening and dependable. Someone who could write, type, and think on her feet. Someone who could help him keep his business in the movement organized. And she had a quirk, a limp when she'd start out walking, like her legs needed to limber up before they worked right. He figured this made her hold back from getting too social, that she didn't have more than a couple of good friends and probably did not have many dates or a love life. After all, she was dull, plain, un-hip, and she seemed to like being that way.

The movement was crying out for a queen like that, and he wanted someone to turn to when he needed a break from the stud life. It was his duty to recruit her.

So he moved in close that evening at Freedom Village. Getting a date with her was easy enough, though she was not the pushover he thought she would be. His attempt to deflect her question about religion disturbed her and almost threw his game off. He had to use the walk to her apartment, away from everybody else, to recover his ground. As he backed away from her door and waited for her to lock herself inside, he imagined schooling her gently in the ways of revolution, giving her just enough of himself to draw her near and keep her in place for his purposes.

The click of her night latch became his signal to turn his attention to other matters. She was now safely tucked away in her apartment and in his mind, and he directed his thoughts toward New Haven Street and the alley behind the shops on the boulevard. Revolutionary business called. He and Marcus exchanged glances and notes during the evening's festivities and slipped away together for a time to make a few phone calls. Now he had to make a run to his old stomping ground where Marcus would be waiting.

Evening had become night, and the breeze had become a chill, westward-moving wind grating against his face and ears. He slipped into his leather jacket, zipped it closed, hunched forward leaning into the wind, and moved briskly, letting the sound of competing sirens form the backdrop for his thoughts. A loud, heavy siren, almost a moan, rumbled closer and closer, and he figured someone was on a crisis ride up to the General. Off in the distance, a shrill, screeching siren, almost a scream, and he figured someone would soon be riding in the back of a police car, on the way to jail.

The wind grew stronger and colder. The chilling air combined with the blare of the sirens and his thoughts about their meaning started to agitate him. Unzipping his jacket, he reached into the inside pocket and retrieved a wool scarf, placing it around his neck and turning up the collar as if to block the sound of the sirens from uncovering memories lurking restlessly behind his eyes.

Chapter 14

For Solly, the *carnaval* slowed time to a shuffle, allowing him to roll back the years to 1955 when he was sixteen. Miles Davis, the Clovers, jazz, and doo-wop rocked his world. The sirens bleated, screeched, and moaned on the night Sunee died, and he tried to replace the sound with the bounce and rhythm of bebop and the sweet whine of a street corner love ballad. The night was clear and star-lit and cold because it was December, with air so cleansed by the wind that the streetlights couldn't dim the delicate, yet steady, glow of stars against the night sky. His brother Rodney had stuck balled-up plugs of toilet paper in his ears, buried his head under the pillow, and pulled the blanket over that.

Solly just lay there in the upper bunk with his hands resting under his head, figuring he'd get little sleep, wondering who was in trouble, what they'd done or even if they'd done anything at all, and if they'd survive to talk about it.

The next morning he discovered the personal meaning that night's sirens would come to symbolize for him. He had managed to fall asleep despite the noise, and the clear night transformed into a cloudy, stormy day. Mixed with the sound of rain steadily hitting the windows and the roof, he heard his grandmother calling on Jesus and moaning loudly, and he heard his grandfather saying things like, "It's bad but it's going to be all right because the boys are already safe, and at least we don't have to go looking for them."

Solly eased down from the upper bunk, noting the whistling snore coming from under the blanket where Rodney's head was still buried. He slipped his pants over his pajamas and crept down the hall toward the living room. Two policemen stood with their hands hanging at their sides, looking in silence at his grandparents with what seemed to Solly to be pity. Somebody had died, and he knew it had to be his mother, Sunee, as he and Rodney called her. That was her club name, her singing name, Sunee Baines. She wasn't Momma or Moms and surely not Mother. She was Sunee, fine Sunee, aiming to make it big with a hit record one day soon. She had good-looking legs that she'd dress up in high leather boots reaching over her knees and stopping just below the short dress that barely covered her butt. "Your mama a whore and I'm-a get me a piece and pass it around," a boy who lived down their street shouted at them. The boy ran, but Solly and Rodney caught up with him and beat him, telling him that if he ever talked about their momma again they'd shove his tongue up his ass.

She rented a flat with two other singers, and even though she lived only a few miles across town from his grandparents' home, they rarely saw her because she seemed to always be on the road. Sometimes she sent postcards from places he read about like New Orleans, San Francisco, New York, and Chicago. But most of the time her postcards came from places in the South, places he never heard of. And he wondered why she never had gigs right there in town. *Gigs.* That was a new word in his vocabulary. A jazz word he heard Miles say during a radio interview. He read somewhere that California was on its way to being the record capital of the world. Maybe rhythm-and-blues singers didn't do real gigs, just country road shows and one-night stands.

"I'll be glad when I get off this hog-maw circuit too," she wrote to him, "but I can't just stick around Hollywood 'cause won't nobody let me in a recording studio. I have to get discovered on the road first."

He pushed his need to see her, to be with her, to walk down the street holding hands with her like he'd seen some mothers and sons do, deep into a far, unlit corner of his mind, the day he found her out. It was earlier that same year, when he heard her voice for the last time. He hadn't planned to try seeing her, unannounced, but the day's events gave him the opportunity. It was visiting Sunday, and just about everybody in his grandparents' small Pentecostal church would ride across town to fellowship with another congregation. "Everybody" included the choir, ushers, preachers, deacons, and whole families, and services would be inside and out, all day.

The congregation caravanned across town in cars, and on the way, Solly knew they were going to pass Sunee's street. Rodney realized it too, and they both stared quietly out the window, trying to see her apartment building. That's when Solly decided to sneak away between services when everybody would be outside eating in the dining tents, listening to gospel music rolling from a record player, and all the children would get the chance to run around and play, including Rodney. In other words, there would be enough distraction for him to leave, unnoticed.

He slipped away as soon as he finished helping with the men folks' duties, setting up tables and chairs, positioning trash cans strategically to receive the throw-away remains of the day's feast, and helping the elderly find seats where they would wait patiently for someone else to serve food to them. He knew his absence wouldn't be noticed until time to help clean up, and he planned to be back by then. He would miss some fried chicken and fish that day but he didn't care. He was determined to pay his mother a surprise visit, and his hope that she'd be home approached being a prayer.

Reaching her building, he could hear blues notes filling the air and he decided to follow the music, figuring it must be from her apartment. He neared, closing in on the sound of voices, a man and a woman talking and laughing. He knocked and a man with a cigarette hanging loosely from his lips answered.

"What you want, little man?"

"Sunee here?"

"What you want her for?"

"She my mama."

"Well, she busy. She can't come to the door."

"Can I come in?"

Then he heard her voice, with a cracking, raspy, softness to it that made him think she might be sick before he realized she was drunk.

"Who that at the door, baby?" she asked.

Solly looked up at the nameless man, who at that moment had the power to keep him from seeing his mother. The man sucked his cigarette once more before removing it from his lips to flick the ashes onto the cement landing.

"Understand me, little man," he said, returning the lit nub to his mouth. "She can't see you now. Maybe later. I'll tell her you stopped by. What's your name?"

Her raspy voice sounded impatient, "Shut the door, baby, and come on back in here."

"Solly. Tell her Solly came to see her," he managed to say as the man closed the door.

Back at church, the singing, shouting, spirit dancing, and preaching of the second service gave him cover for his tears.

And on that morning when he was sixteen, he figured she was dead and he knew even without the details that her death had to have been hard and painful.

"She's in the morgue at the General," he heard the policeman say to his folks.

"Is Sunee Baines her full name?" the policeman asked."

"No, suh. Geraldine Etta Baines. That's her real name. Put that on your paper, suh."

As Solly walked back to the bedroom, he heard the policemen offer to take his grandparents up to the General to claim Sunee's body and find out more about how she died. He sat on the floor and leaned his head on Rodney's bunk. There he waited for their grandpa to come tell them the news.

Through the blackness on his first night in Puerto de Vida he saw occasional lights on the hillside dimly flicker, then disappear, and then flicker again. It reminded him of the night he walked Loretha home and eased closer to her need for a man's touch. The street lights flickered, and the aging lamp posts bent and swayed in the wind. After he left her, he walked fast, almost jogged over to the edge of an alley behind Oasis Boulevard. There he stood under another aging streetlight, eyeing the abandoned field across the way. He thought it ironic how the plot of land, seemingly devoid of life, kept demanding his attention. *People would always call that lot "vacant" as if it didn't have boarded-up houses on it,* he thought.

Four of them, empty, painted lime green and sunset orange by somebody who liked to smack your vision with loud, funky colors. Then whoever did it moved away, he guessed, because nobody had ever lived in those houses as long as he could remember. His grandma said she heard gangsters owned them back in the late forties. The houses were boarded up ever since there was a shootout with the police. But his grandpa said that was all gossip, and he thought it was a damn shame somebody would let perfectly good land go to waste like that.

It seemed to Solly there were always people trying to get rid of those houses, because to grown folks, they were eyesores where a whole lot of shady stuff would go on right under everybody's nose. Soon after Professor Howard moved her bookstore to that big two-story house on the corner of Oasis Boulevard and New Haven Street, she even started a campaign to get the houses demolished, going around knocking on people's doors, talking them into signing petitions for her to take down to

City Hall. And Marcus would usually be right behind her when she went on one of her petition-signing campaigns.

The first time Solly saw Marcus, he was trailing behind Professor Howard, carrying a big clipboard with stacks of paper fastened under its large clamps. Solly was already in high school by then and didn't pay much attention to Marcus, figuring any homeboy who followed his momma around like that must be a chump. But Rodney took notice. He said he saw Marcus throw down some hard licks on that same boy they beat up for playing the dozens on their momma a couple of years earlier.

"He don't fight like no sissy neither," Rodney told him. "And he's always got money too. Maybe his momma pays him to be her flunky."

"If she got to pay him, she's his fool. He's getting over on her," Solly said. "Can you picture Gramps telling us to do something and then paying us?"

"Aw, hell naw," Rodney said. "We'd get an ass-kicking if we even look like we want some money."

Solly hung back and observed while Rodney and Marcus became good friends, but since Solly wasn't sure what Marcus was made of, he told Rodney not to let his new buddy know that they played around in those houses. Anyway he was glad his little brother and the well-off boy from a few blocks away were tight with each other, because after a while, Professor Howard warmed up to Rodney and to him. Once she became accustomed to their visits to see Marcus, she asked them what kind of magazines they liked to read. Her mouth dropped when they told her they only liked comic books, but lo and behold, one day Solly went to meet Rodney at the bookshop, and there on the magazine rack was a row of detective and superhero comics. Still, Solly didn't want Marcus hanging around when they were in those houses, so he made Rodney promise not to tell.

Occasionally the windows in those old houses were nailed shut like somebody tried to secure them from intruders, and at other times Solly and Rodney lifted up the wood and climbed right inside playing around until they figured their grandpa was out scouting the neighborhood for them. Then they'd leave, run through the alley behind Mr. Leonardo's pawnshop and over to New Haven Street to meet their grandpa in the middle of the block as if they were coming from the church playground.

Grandpa Baines's warning not to let him catch them in that field came echoing back to him, and he had to chuckle because it was never enough to keep them away, not even when they got caught and knew they'd get a whipping.

That's what happened the day Rodney broke his leg. Solly was only twelve when they discovered the basement in one of the houses. They never noticed it from the outside because the basement window was covered with weeds and tall grass.

Rodney was the one who jimmied open the kitchen door leading down, and they both peered in, each daring the other to descend into that dark hole. Then they stopped daring and started bargaining. "I'll go if you do." So Solly ventured in first and Rodney followed. When they reached the bottom of the stairs, fear overtook their curiosity. Rodney swore he heard a growl, and Solly insisted he smelled something foul, like an animal, dead and rotting. Scampering back up, Rodney caught his foot in a hole in one of the steps they had carefully avoided on their way down.

But instead of stopping to remove his foot, he simply yanked it forward and fell deeper into the hole. Now his leg was in up to the knee. Solly pulled as hard as he could to get him free and then pushed him up the stairs. Everybody for blocks around must have heard Rodney screaming when they ran from that house, and somebody must have alerted their grandpa because he met them on the corner. It was times like that that Grandpa Baines called him by his whole name.

"Solomon Odell Baines, didn't I tell you not to play around in them shacks? And look, you let your little brother get hurt."

For Solly, Rodney made the years growing up without Sunee bearable and fun. That forsaken piece of earth with its abandoned houses became their rough hideaway, and as they grew, "fun" became teenaged daring. They lost their fear and explored more of their underground hideout, discovering a tunnel between the houses and a second basement. They cleaned up one of the basements and sealed one end of the tunnel so nobody could get in but them. There they smoked cigarettes stolen from Grandpa Baines, and they smoked weed too when they could get their hands on it. With their own hiding place, they could stay clear of the junkies and the transients, because Solly and Rodney weren't the only ones breaking into those houses. Fun and daring belonged in their youth, in the dawning of their manliness when they were bad-assed and naive at the same time.

The days and months of their youth became years, and the field and the houses with secret tunnels formed the kind of memories they could reminisce about as they grew. Solly graduated from high school and set his sights on learning a trade—small electronics and radio and television repair—so he could leave his grandparents' home to live like a Player. He spelled "Player" with a capital "P" because all through his school years, girls liked him. His grandmother wanted him to find a nice church-going girl, the way his mother used to be until his father came along and ruined her by telling her he could make her a famous singer and then dumping her for somebody else.

"All he left her with was you and your brother," Grandma Baines told Solly. "A busted heart and an itch for the streets that stole her life away. You don't want to be like your daddy. He was no good, that's for sure."

Grandma Baines was more than a little anxious for him to settle down, but his grandpa told him he had plenty of time for that. Since the country wasn't caught up in a big war, he ought to join the military so he could see some of what's happening in the world beyond Desert Haven and the big city it was part of. But the choice wasn't really in Solly's hands, because he hadn't even finished trade school when he got drafted into the army and sent overseas. There, he worked on radios and other electronic devices. He liked being away from home, but the only thing he liked about military life was his time off, when he could go looking for whiskey and women along with the other soldiers.

In 1962, when his tour of duty was just about over, he got a letter from Rodney saying he'd joined the Marines and to hurry up back home so he could see him before he shipped off to Southeast Asia. *Damn, that's just like Rodney,* Solly thought. *Itching to get away from Gramps so bad he'd walk into a war.*

Rodney was the reason Solly went back into their basement hideout again. It was in 1965, after Rodney had come back from Vietnam in a flag-covered casket and they buried him next to Sunee. It was after Solly sat home with his grandparents while a host of folks from their church and from the neighborhood came by to pay their respects.

Professor Howard came too. She told everybody how much her Marcus had loved Rodney, and when he got back from college, how much he would miss hanging out with his brave friend. After all the reminiscing about Rodney the boy, Rodney the man, and Rodney the Marine quieted down and everybody left, after his grandpa drank a little gin to help escape his sorrow and his grandma prayed herself to sleep, Solly slipped away and over to the field. He went back to their boyhood hideout and slumped on the floor, tears stinging his cheeks, while visions of Rodney the kid laughed and clowned before his eyes. And through his sobs, loud bursts of laughter escaped from him that night as he wished he could wrestle his little brother to the floor, whack him on the back of his head, and chase him up those dilapidated stairs once more.

Rodney's death made Solly look toward his grandparents for solace, but in that gaze, he saw them, for the first time, as old and weary. They could do little to relieve his suffering, for they were no longer the strong, invincible folks who raised him. It seemed to him that losing Rodney hurt so bad they aged under the burden of it. They got tired more often, were quieter, and their smiles seemed painted in place, automatic; these changes sobered him.

Solly fixed up the back house on their property, empty since the last tenant because his grandpa had gotten slow about doing the repairs, and he moved in to keep watch over them. Before he did that, he made money from the streets, selling anything that would bring him some folding green—anything, that is, except a woman's body. Doing that didn't fit his Player image. He gambled, ran the numbers for a betting ring, sold bootleg cigarettes and liquor, and even worked at a regular job, but only if he had to. He lived cheaply when money was short but partied as hard as he could even when broke.

After he decided to look after his folks, he got a real job in a radio and TV repair shop, yet that didn't stop him from maintaining his hustle, from making money in the underground economy fixing people's radios, televisions, electrical wiring and getting paid only in cash. Although he quit gambling and running numbers, he sold weed on the side from time to time, in small amounts so he wouldn't become known or watched as a dealer. He didn't stop chasing women though, and he wouldn't allow one to call him her boyfriend for more than two months before disappearing from her life.

It took his brother's getting blown up by a land mine to make Solly peer into the well of his own sadness and rage. Questions spun upward from his depths, rattling in his head like seeds in a gourd, and he decided to face them. The question about why Rodney died—and the simple answer that he joined the Man's war and ran out of luck chasing an enemy somebody else chose for him—didn't satisfy Solly's need to know. He questioned why so many ordinary guys who looked like Rodney and who, like him, were sent to die in faraway countries, yet here in the States got their asses systematically kicked when the Man needed to unleash some rage on somebody, and were excluded when there was anything good to go around. His looking inward caused him to search for answers, to begin reading, and to begin earnestly listening and seeking.

He went into the New World Bookshop and Culture Center and bought a recording of Malcolm X's speech, "The Ballot or the Bullet." While he made his purchase, he thought what a shame he'd waited too late to hear him in person, for Malcolm was dead by the time Solly started to soak in his message. As he thumbed through the books the professor had by King, he had trouble deciding what to read first, and he ended the argument with himself by choosing the earliest ones, *Stride toward Freedom* and *The Measure of a Man*.

In the evenings, after returning to his backyard cottage from a day hustling or working, he'd listen to Malcolm's recording, read King's books way into the night, and he'd bounce between the two, trying to see which message held the most truth for him. Back out on the street, he stopped ignoring the activism around him and started looking directly at the folks his age who were acting out, marching, organizing, protesting, getting people to the polls to vote under threat of death, burning draft cards, fleeing the country, and taking the nation on a wild train ride it didn't want to be part of but seemed powerless to stop.

But his questions about the trouble in his own life really didn't begin with Rodney, the war, or the country's upheaval. Roiling up from his gut were unanswered questions and grief about Sunee's death, why her boyfriend dropped her off at the General and left her to die alone, screaming through her drunkenness that her stomach hurt. Why the doctors and nurses waited so long to get to her, letting her appendix explode inside, silencing her forever. And why they lied to his grandparents, saying she died of a drug overdose, until the autopsy results exposed them.

So Solly got up one morning, thinking of heroes and what they said about being prepared and getting an education, and figured that was a good place for him to make some more changes in his life. It was one of the main ideas Malcolm and King agreed on: trained minds and skilled hands. He checked on his grandparents, quit his job, and headed up to State looking for answers. Two months later, he'd gotten into college using his GI benefits.

That's when he joined the revolution.

For Solly, the meaning of that field and abandoned houses changed after Rodney died and he said good-bye to him in the basement away from everyone else. They became invisible, a seemingly empty space in the middle of the boulevard he'd drive by and deliberately ignore. They stayed that way for a while, nonthings, until April 4, 1968, when he reasoned that some of the people involved in the goings-on that night would need a hiding place. But Professor Howard pulled a wild card from a deck he'd forgotten she was holding, and that field was about to change again.

On that late October night, after walking Loretha home, Solly allowed the thoughts of New World Books and Culture Center and of Loretha to fade from his mind. The boulevard was quiet with only a few cars passing now and then. Solly hunched his shoulders up once more against the wind, crossed the street, stepped easily over the broken fence, and walked toward the back of the house where a lone man waited.

Solly's car waited too, parked between the house and the massive, sagging oak tree leaning toward the structure, its burdened branches mingling with untended oleander and wild ivy. As he walked past Marcus, he reached down to retrieve the car keys being held out for him and in a soldierly way, grabbed Marcus's forearm and pulled him up.

"Put that cigarette out, man." Solly said. He waited while Marcus took one more drag, dropped the cigarette to the ground, crushed and spit on it, and then crushed it some more.

Solly led, moving cautiously into the house before turning on the flashlight, aiming the beam toward the floor so as little light as possible escaped the room. Quietly and quickly they moved, locating four heavy, locked metal containers, and two suitcases, much lighter in weight, hidden in the narrow tunnel between the basements of the houses. They took turns removing them. One would be the lookout, while the other loaded a container into the car's trunk. When they finished, Solly slid into the driver's seat and motioned for Marcus to hurry. He didn't turn on the headlights until they were back on the boulevard going toward the freeway.

That night marked the first time Solly laid eyes on the metal containers and the suitcases, but he didn't have to ask Marcus what they held. He instinctively knew. As they drove, he started marching mentally backward through events placing him next to Marcus in a car with a trunkload of weapons and other people's money that could get them life in a federal prison if they were caught.

"Brother King's death is propitious," Marcus told him on April 4, a few hours after the killing in Memphis. "We gonna do this thing tonight. You with us, bro?"

He slowly rotated a cigarette between his thumb and forefinger as he spoke, then took a long, hard drag, blew the smoke from his nostrils, and let little ringlets of it float from his mouth.

"Naw, man. I'll show you how to get into them tunnels," Solly said, "but I ain't gonna be down with you on the street tonight."

Solly said this standing head to head with Marcus, who had a way of looking ferocious when he wasn't around Professor Howard. In her presence, he saw Marcus as the dutiful son, the southside good boy, but away from her, he'd transform into Marcus the revolutionary, Marcus, the gun-toting, cigarette-smoking avenger, exacting pounds of flesh and whatever else he could from the system that had done nothing while his grandfather's store was fire bombed and his uncle burned alive.

"You scared?" Marcus asked him.

"Ain't scared for you or me," Solly said. "Scared for what could happen to innocent people if you and your crew mess up."

"Aw, man, you just a jive-assed, armchair revolutionary. When you gonna put your money where your mouth is?" Marcus said.

"People have to be ready for revolution, and most people I know ain't." Then he added, "You ain't either. What you gonna do if you get caught?"

"If the pigs catch me, it'll be on account of somebody snitched," Marcus said.

"Ain't nothing I want from them devils bad enough to help them catch black people," Solly said. "You haven't answered me, man. What you gonna do if you get caught?"

"O ye of little faith. I ain't getting caught, bro. Ain't no sense in having a backup plan for something that ain't gonna happen."

That Marcus was bold enough to rob a bank didn't surprise Solly. What got on his nerves was that Marcus was arrogant and calculating, and in a hurry to put a hurt on somebody. And how Marcus was able to fool Professor Howard proved mystifying. She completely believed the tale he told her about ripping his thigh on a loose fence wire while trying to help some people out of a burning house the night of the revolt. For days, she kept saying how brave he was, just like his father and her father. Solly was glad she got preoccupied with building Freedom Village and all that talk died down. He figured Marcus must have been glad she stopped too.

A smirk crossed Solly's face as he drove down the freeway when he thought about Marcus sticking that revolver in his side pants pocket and the thing discharging, the bullet grazing his leg while he ran from the bank. The professor really doesn't know her son, he thought. But then if she did, what would she do about it? What could she do?

Solly realized, long before the happenings of that April evening, that Marcus was a liability. Early on, he came to the Brotherhood meetings talking about ramping up the revolution and reciting a litany of abuses his family suffered in the South before he was born. He rambled on about how his father, whom he'd never seen in person, was killed in World War II and his remains sent to Texas instead of California, how he rode beside his mother on a segregated train when they went back to claim what was left of his father, and how he watched and listened when she was called auntie by the army officer in charge and treated like a child instead of a grown woman. And when somebody in the meetings would try to shut him up by saying everybody there had a story like his and that the question was how to set things straight, he'd always have the same answer.

"Time to blow up some shit."

Solly decided it was useless wishing he and Marcus weren't caught between two poles of the same movement. Solly had no quarrel with militant agitation, but not all-out armed urban warfare. Overseas, he'd seen firsthand what those with power would do to crush the powerless. He saw, too, flashing on the news every day from places like Vietnam, the Middle East, and Angola, what the powerless would do to fight back, using themselves, their own children and their elders as weapons. He had to honestly admit he wasn't ready for that kind of violence where the streets of Desert Haven could become a deadly theater of war, with the skyscrapers of the city beyond as its backdrop.

When Solly's thoughts delved into all the movements revolving around him, the words in his head could switch from everyday-black-brother parlance and flow from his mouth with often comical revolutionary fervor. He identified it as his inner warrior, the part of himself that had finally found something to get excited about.

In a fit of rhetorical passion one night, Solly told the Brotherhood that black power would become a beacon of light for oppressed people the world over, but it wouldn't be easy. If black folks were going to lead the charge, they would have to prove they had what it takes to make revolutionary change.

"Unity," he said. "Stepping together, ya'll dig it?" Then he waited for a reaction, and after seeing a few affirmative nods, he continued.

"Power to the people," he said.

But he felt that Marcus, at the opposite end of the spectrum and arming himself and anybody else who would listen for battle, had to be managed, and that meant covering for him.

"I got your back now, man, but it's the last time," he told Marcus on April 4, 1968, just after nightfall. Solly handed Marcus a diagram of the basements and told him where best to enter without being seen from the street.

"If you get caught, you're on your own, you and that secret army you hooked up with," Solly told him.

"What're you and the Brotherhood gonna be up to when things really start going down?" Marcus asked.

"Stuff is already happening, and we got to get as many stranded people, especially old folks and kids, off the streets as we can."

After that conversation, Solly drove to New World Bookshop and Culture Center, leaving Marcus standing across the street from the field, studying the diagram.

When the rap session ended, Solly went straight to his grandparents' home. He told them to stay in the back rooms of the house and to keep the curtains closed and the front rooms dark. They didn't question why, and he figured since they already smelled the smoke and heard the sirens and the gunshots in the distance, they didn't need to ask.

His second destination was to the narrow side street between Serrano Avenue and New Haven. The street was anchored by a church at each end, New Haven Baptist on the north and *Iglesia de Los Santos* on the south. There, he rendezvoused with other members of the Brotherhood. They decided to ride in teams of two, each team taking a section of Desert Haven to cruise, looking for stranded residents to pick up and deliver to their homes or to one of the two churches. Solly told them to keep copious notes on their whereabouts that evening, the time they were in specific places, and who they talked to. Above all, get the names of the people they helped and a phone number if possible.

"We ain't gonna have time for all that," Angelo said.

"Well, do what you can. When the cops start throwing people in jail for looting, we'll all need alibis we can prove."

"I thought Marcus would be rolling with us tonight," Jerome said.

"I thought so too," Solly said, "but he ain't nowhere around and we can't wait. That means I have to ride solo."

The Brotherhood got lucky on April 4 though. None of them was picked up for looting, at least not during the revolt or its immediate aftermath.

That October night months later, when Solly found himself driving down the freeway with stolen money and weapons in his car, all he could do was hope the police weren't watching. He suspected that the law was already hip to Marcus, but he wasn't sure Marcus could see the danger or was too much of a fool to really care.

"You know, man," Solly said as they headed south on the 405. "You got trouble hanging around you."

"What you talking 'bout, man?" Marcus asked, lighting another cigarette.

"I mean, people you don't know very well."

"Who, Spoon? He just a book freak like Loretha. He cool."

"Watch him, he smells like an undercover cop to me. He came from nowhere and he's trying to move in too close."

"Tell you what," Marcus said. "Why don't you pull him into the Brotherhood and keep him busy with teach-ins and crap like that while I do my real revolutionary thing, okay?"

"He ain't getting in the Brotherhood. I'll make sure of that," Solly said. "You just better figure out how to keep him from digging any deeper into your business."

They drove for miles that night, mostly in silence. When they reached the outskirts of the county, they pulled behind an auto repair shop. They were met there by one of Solly's old army buddies, Jim, the only white soldier he'd gotten really close to. Jim went underground when he returned to the States, growing weed and fixing cars. He wore his hair long and sported a beard and sideburns so thick they nearly covered his whole face.

They talked for a few minutes and then moved from the shadows into the light of the shop. Solly pulled a map from his jacket and the two men studied it. Jim drew lines charting a route that would lead them into a remote desert area. No smiles were exchanged, but when they finished, they touched knuckles and linked hands as if to seal their secret, and Jim followed up with the peace sign. The whole time this was going on, Marcus watched the two of them and surveyed the shop like he was looking for someone or something.

"Hey, man," Marcus shouted at Jim. "I know you got some weed. Where's your stash at, huh?"

"No time for that, Marcus. Let's go," Solly said.

They traded Solly's car for a pickup truck, loaded it with their cargo and carefully covered the containers and two shovels with heavy canvas and tied them all down with rope. Then after changing into jeans, donning cowboy boots and hats and hooking an American flag to the truck's CB radio antenna, they headed southeast toward the desert.

Back home a day later, Solly answered his phone just before dawn. He could hear sirens in the distance as he talked. When the call ended, he slipped on his pants and walked outside, stepping like a cat along the path from the backyard to the front until he reached the edge of his grandparents' house. There he stood in the shadows between the porch and the large jacaranda tree, its branches swaying languidly in the early morning breeze, and watched black smoke rising from the field on Oasis Boulevard.

By the time he checked on his folks a while later, the abandoned houses and everything living in and around them on that plot of ground had burned into the earth. In Solly's mind, the field now settled back into its place as a nonthing.

On the Saturday following Thanksgiving, 1968, nearly a month after Freedom Village opened and after the fire in the field, Solly walked along the path to his cottage and felt an urge to see Grandma and Grandpa Baines. He tried to dismiss the feeling, noting that it was still dark, too early, and he didn't want to wake them. Still, even as he reasoned they were asleep, he placed his briefcase next to his door and walked toward their house, letting himself in through the back entrance. He tip-toed toward the dim shaft of light in the hall, and realized that the lamp was on in their room, too. Solly rarely ever approached his folks when they were in their room, let alone that early in the morning, but the feeling that he needed to see them was no longer a desire but an imperative. Even before he laid eyes on them, the meaning of his actions and feelings had become clear.

He'd heard about older couples, married for so long they seemed forever bound, dying within days, hours, even minutes of one another. He sat on the floor and looked at them and after some moments, talked to them. And when he'd looked and talked enough, he did what he thought they'd want him to do. He called their minister to come pray over them before calling the mortuary to come take them away.

Chapter 15

It occurred to Solly that Califa was bonafide proof women do lead revolutions. In his mind, she must have been a hell of a revolutionary to drive all those bloodthirsty, women-hungry conquerors away from her turf. Back in the day before slaves were brought to the Western Hemisphere, there must have been a real Califa, ferocious and swift to fight if riled, but mellow when she wanted to be, and so fine and free she molded herself into a myth. But wholesale slavery never took hold in the land that became California. Maybe she's the one who got in the way of the slave peddlers, like Loretha got in the way of that bastard Bernard and exposed him.

He even told Loretha that Califa was a hell of a revolutionary, but when he started swearing that Califa must have been real flesh, blood, and bones at one time, Loretha looked at him as if all that talk of revolution was starting to unhinge his reasoning power.

"I wonder how Califa died." he said, "If she went out fighting, defending what was hers, or if she went down slow, worn from old age and all that fooling around she did when she was young and fine."

Solly's mind had two tracks for women. They were good or bad, strong or weak. The good, strong ones he placed on pedestals, and that's where he placed Loretha, almost without thinking, somewhere no one else could touch her, so he thought.

Solly saw that Loretha's revolution included allies from across the usual barriers dividing people according to class and race just as his did, and how she handled them was another way she surprised him.

Late one afternoon in July, 1974, he left a gathering of his own allies, a group of wealthy social justice liberals. They paid him some good money to stand in front of a microphone and talk to them while they ate lunch, and he was riding on a mild high about the check he would take to the bank the next day. Half of it would go to the Brotherhood's Freedom Fund, though, to pay the cadre of lawyers Roy had hired to handle all the cases stemming from the mass arrests that went down on the south side.

As he drove toward the coalition office to pick up Loretha, he passed the General, where he saw a long line of folks with picket signs promoting everything from ending war to labor rights for custodians and nurses, as well as free medical care for everybody. When he arrived, he parked his car a short distance from the office. As he approached, he eyed a small crowd milling around the door, peering in at something going on. He walked by them and entered the building looking for Loretha. He found her, standing and leaning against the back wall of the reception area with her arms folded across her chest. A man stood facing her a few feet away. He had one hand in his jacket pocket and held a fat manila folder under his other arm.

Loretha looked past the man and at Solly. In that second, he guessed whose back he was approaching. He stopped walking for an instant and then continued, stopping again when he reached the man's side and turned to look at his profile.

"What do you want from my woman?" Solly said.

"Excuse me?" CJ asked, not taking his eyes off Loretha.

Lottie, nervous about the whole scene, tried to ease the tension by blurting out CJ's name and saying he was coming over to their side because he wanted to help. Solly didn't seem at all impressed, and his nostrils flared as CJ finally turned his head to the side to look him in the eye.

"I'm Clay Bernard, Miss Emmitt's doctor. I'm here to see my patient."

"What if she doesn't want to see you?"

"That would be a shame because I have her medical records, and I know what happened to her."

"Since when did the General start sending slave doctors out to treat the field hands?"

"I'm no house slave. The folks at the General didn't send me and will call the cops when they figure out what I've done."

Revolutions never cease, Solly thought.

Solly had no regrets that September in Puerto De Vida when he thought about the way he moved, almost without conscious intent, into Loretha's revolution, using it to absorb his thoughts, taking his attention away from his own struggles.

When he saw that she wasn't going to back away from the General without a fight and that she planned to confront everybody who had anything to do with what happened to her, he decided to follow her lead. He tripped about it at first. She had always been the one in the background, asking questions when they were alone and being politely quiet in public on official movement business, speaking only when spoken to.

He could see she wasn't as shy as she appeared though, just watchful. She would let her eyes survey and land on whatever stirred her curiosity, and she'd observe the details of the happenings of the moment and scribble about them later in that journal she kept. He knew she really accepted him as her man when she started leaving the journal out on the nightstand instead of sticking it between the headboard and the wall on her side of the bed. It's like she didn't care if he picked it up and read it, yet he knew she trusted he wouldn't. He figured he didn't need to sneak a look, though. He could ask her what was in it and she'd read it to him.

His revolution started falling apart with deep ideological differences and mistrust, splintering people into factions and bringing the movement to a standstill, because nobody could agree on a program of action. Revolutionary groups that should have been working together were instead shooting at each other with the same kind of weapons Reverend Gilliam railed about at Junebug's funeral. The night Marcus disappeared, things got so heated at the United Revolutionary Vanguard's Desert Haven headquarters, Solly thought he was going to have to pull out his piece and shoot somebody to keep from taking a bullet himself.

They fought over tactics. All branches of the Vanguard agreed on one thing: to start some action in key California cities at the same time. The cities discussed were San Diego, Fresno, Los Angeles, Oakland, and Sacramento, but the branches couldn't agree on what the action should be. Different branches argued with each other, and members within each branch fought as well. Some of the members in the Desert Haven wing of the movement wanted to plan and carry out skirmishes with the police. But Solly said that was crazy. Black people would not support anything that looked like all-out guerilla warfare, and they would be the first to turn on them.

"Naw, they won't," somebody shouted. "When they see we're fighting for them, they'll protect us. The pigs won't know who to go after."

"Which means they'll target everybody, women and children included, and do the same things to us they did to the Native Americans and are doing right now everywhere else they can get away with it," Solly shouted back.

"You just chicken-shit, Solly man. You're supposed to be revolutionary, but you just plain scared. Ain't that right, Marcus?"

Before Marcus could respond, Solly yelled back.

"I ain't scared and I damn sure ain't stupid. What have we done to gain the people's trust? What have we shown them except we know how to light up the neighborhoods with bullets just like the street gangs, huh? Most folks already think we ain't nothing but a bunch of thugs."

"So what you got in your bag, Solly? What you think we ought to do?"

"We got to stop fighting each other. That's our biggest problem. We ain't united. When folks see us sticking together, they'll get behind us. Anyway, most of our people are comfortable in their oppression. They ain't giving up none of that comfort as long as we look like gangsters instead of freedom fighters."

"What else can we do, man? We already feeding the poor down there at the Village and going to bat for them with the cops. They're starting to come to us more than they go to the NAACP when they got a beef with the law. I hope you ain't talking about all that marching again, 'cause I ain't doing that."

"They don't see us," Marcus yelled. "They see my momma. Professor Howard feeds the poor. Professor Howard's got a freedom school. Professor Howard's putting the heat on the cops. They don't see us. They see my momma." Marcus jumped up and pushed chairs out of his way as he shouted, and as he ran down the hall toward the back of the building, he yelled out a warning. "They out to get us. Y'all better wake up 'cause they coming."

Marcus ran into the bathroom and Solly heard the lock click after him. By the time Solly and the others broke the lock and entered, Marcus had managed to squeeze himself out through the bathroom window. "Wonder why that fool didn't just leave out the back door," Solly thought out loud.

He left to look for Marcus and the meeting went on without him, but not for long. When he returned, alone, the place was dark.

Solly knew that a lot of the mistrust and indecision in the revolution was the work of outsiders, informants, and undercover cops. The civil rights movement, with all its problems, still managed to make the country look at and question itself, so the FBI set up its own secret wing to infiltrate and destroy that movement and the revolution. They were both seen by the establishment as dangerous, and everybody involved knew they were being targeted, manipulated, and watched.

The machinations of the police and the FBI taught Solly to keep his mind on full alert all the time. This was the tension behind how he looked out at the world and the way the world saw him. He perfected the art of the blank, undecipherable stare even before his hustler days, when he and Rodney had to be wary of the cops as well as of their grandpa. They didn't know who'd be watching as they slipped into those old, abandoned houses on Oasis Boulevard.

He trained himself to sense when someone walked behind him even before he heard footsteps or when someone across a room or across the street followed him with watchful eyes and suspicious actions, allowing him to identify where they lurked. He learned to smell a cop, even if she was dressed like a sister revolutionary or he was splayed out like a drunk on a street corner. He learned the smells of the people he knew and hung around with. That's how he could tell Loretha where she'd been on a given day if he should happen to walk into a place that she'd left. Her scent, he followed. Other smells made him hang back and instinctively take on the stealth of a tiger, quiet his steps, ready his weapon for firing, and breathe in the scent of the danger so he'd know how and when to confront it.

His instinct told him a few weeks after the URV meeting that Marcus was back and waiting for him. Solly had just returned to his apartment, late, and had driven behind the building into the garage. The alley was quiet except for the sound of his car's engine and the squeak of the door as he opened and closed it. Large, cardboard storage boxes were stacked against a pillar, and barely three feet of space separated the boxes from the wall. When his boot hit the cement floor, a whiff of a familiar scent, mixed with the odor of someone who hadn't bathed in a while, made him turn his head toward the pillar and the boxes. Marcus. Solly's instincts didn't tell him what mood Marcus was in, so he took out his gun, all the while hoping he wouldn't have to shoot Professor Howard's only son.

"Come from behind those boxes, Marcus. I know you're back there."

Solly's command stirred only an alley cat, which ran from the garage and disappeared into the street. He released the safety on the gun, and the loud click reverberated against the concrete walls and the quiet of the night. He got a response.

"Don't shoot, man. I ain't packing."

Marcus crawled from behind the boxes and pulled himself up, slowly, using the pillar for support. The odor of sweat, mingled with the stench of stale food and urine, saturated his clothes, the same ones he wore at the URV meeting. Seeing this bad-assed revolutionary brought so low made Solly inhale deep to smell it all as a reminder of what carelessness could do to even him if he weren't vigilant.

"Help me bro, I ain't got nowhere else to turn. Spoon set me up, man. He's a damn pig."

Solly looked around and then put his gun away and helped Marcus up the back stairs to his apartment. He deposited him on the bathroom floor, turned on the water in the tub, threw a towel at him, and told him not to leave the bathroom until he'd cleaned himself up.

Solly realized he needed to get Marcus out of the country and that Marcus couldn't go alone. So Solly spent the rest of the night deciding which of his underground allies were trustworthy enough to call on for help and what Marcus and he would need in terms of money and vehicles to carry off the escape.

So the trip through the South was for Marcus. Solly's contacts supplied them with new driver's licenses, fake passports, and new identities. They disguised themselves as black peasants, migrant workers at times and preachers at others, and rode for hundreds of miles through Arizona and Texas in the back of pickup trucks and old taxi cabs before reaching the border and slipping into Mexico.

Being on the road with Marcus, who slid back and forth between fright and rage about the mess he was in, made Solly feel as though he was literally navigating his way through hell. Marcus was hard to manage, even on that trip, because, as Solly figured, part of his mind had already dipped into madness. Marcus was, Solly believed, close to losing the rest of his mind completely. But Solly didn't feel he had a choice. He had to help him.

The trip reminded him of the night he showed Marcus where to hide the bank's money and the cases of guns and bullets. He did it then because even though he knew Marcus was foolish and dangerous, he didn't want him to get caught. Now, he opted to help him escape because he felt if the cops caught him, they'd lynch him on the spot. He probably wouldn't even make it to trial, but if he did, it wouldn't be a fair one. Those prospects enraged Solly, and his intense need to get over on the system once again trumped his fear of getting caught. Besides, he rationalized, Professor Howard didn't deserve any of this, and she certainly didn't deserve to have her son lynched. He silenced what little guilt he felt by telling himself he was doing it for her.

But Solly didn't get things right with Loretha before he left, didn't concoct a believable story that would satisfy her curiosity. He didn't want her to know the truth, because that would have been dangerous, and he trusted she'd believe him without much struggle when he got back. After all, she had never been mad at him for too long in the past. He didn't think this time would be any different.

An urgent need to be with her, to touch her, and to draw strength from her serenity hit hard and stayed with him on that trip. But when he showed up again, safely, relieved to be back, she surprised him. She let him inside her and wrestled with him, facing off with him with fury he didn't realize she could call up. Yet she pushed him away at the same time. He knew after a while that what bothered her wasn't that she thought he had been with another woman; for a change, he hadn't. What bothered her were the frayed threads of their relationship, stretched and worn and about to break. He knew she wanted trust and honesty in a bad way. But he didn't realize until she finally challenged him, refused to go along with his demands, that he didn't have much of either quality in reserve to call on. He was just as flawed as he accused his brothers in the movement of being. He was relieved when Professor Howard rescued his ass and got Loretha and him back together, and he mentally thanked her. His mind paused after that thought, listening to the heavy beat of the next one, the other matter he had to clear with the professor before their trip to Puerto de Vida that September ended. He struggled, though, with how and when to tell her. He hoped a good opportunity would present itself, and he settled, almost lazily, into that hope. Professor Howard ended his indecision. She confronted him.

"Solly, I have to know. Where is Marcus?"

They were on the beach together, just the two of them.

"Marcus is alive," he told her. "The underground helped me get him into Mexico. He realized too late that one of his so-called brothers in the struggle was an undercover cop. Marcus was set up to take blame for the bank robbery. I went with him through Arizona and Texas and into Mexico. We didn't try to cross the California border, because we figured more cops would be looking for us there. That's why it took so long. Another runner took over in Mexico, and we just had to trust it was a real revolutionary soldier and not another undercover cop."

"But where is he now?"

"He's in a village in Belize."

"He really did it, didn't he," she said, looking at him over the edges of her glasses. It was the look

Loretha described to him as Professor Howard's Earth Momma stare. "Yeah," Solly said. "But he said he didn't shoot the guard, and I believe him. The snitch did all the shooting." Then he added, "Marcus had to run. He'd never get a fair trial, you know," and his voice trailed up like a question, a plea for her to understand.

"I might not ever see him again," she said, looking away and past him toward the ocean and then turning her head to the sky with her eyes closed.

"You might not. But he wants you to know that he loves you and misses you, and he's sorry he didn't live up to the dreams you had for him."

Solly held out his hand to her and then watched her turn and walk away from him, not bothering to lift her long skirt so it wouldn't drag in the sand. She moaned, a deep moan, rolling up from the ground beneath their feet, and he thought the earth was about to shake. When she turned toward him again he had already opened his arms wide to receive her. She ran and threw herself at him and let him hold her while she screamed and laughed and cried like he did when he lost Rodney.

Part III

❧

September 1977
Puerto de Vida, Mexico
CJ Remembers

Chapter 16

Puerto de Vida beaches reminded Claymore Earnest Bernard Jr.—Clay to family, CJ to friends—of the ones he had seen along the west coast of Africa, where the beaches were pocked with centuries-old castles hiding dungeons for captured human beings headed for slavery. He saw the castles back in 1965 when he and Dolores were in the Peace Corps. They kissed and held each other close on those beaches each time they walked through a castle and out into the sunlight again.

The smell and feel of Puerto de Vida's beaches weren't much different from those of West Africa, but here the castles were cliffs, shaved and shaped by water and wind and standing tall above moist, sandy earth. As in Africa, the nights were heavy with unseen life and mystery.

He left Dolores and Malakia asleep in the cottage that first night in Puerto de Vida and moved slowly down the wooden steps from the top of the cliff to the beach below. His hips and knees, stiff from the long ride down the coast, urged him to jog as soon as his feet landed on sand. His body moved forward quickly. His mind kept up. On the surface of his thoughts and actions, he was there in Puerto de Vida to cut loose and to leave his troubles behind and have a good time, yet he stared as if compelled by unnamed forces into the night surrounding him, searching for signs of his father, whom he hadn't seen in seven years.

CJ was obsessed, but he knew that walking along the beach would bring him solace. It was meditation for him. He didn't call it that, but the sound of his steps on the sand, and the swish and slap of the waves against the shore cleared his head of thoughts. When his own voice stringing words together in his mind reappeared, its presence was calm and logical. It wasn't the blackness that soothed him like it did Solly. It was the quiet hum he'd hear when the words left his mind.

The realization that he wouldn't find his father in Puerto de Vida led him to silently admit that he'd always been looking for him, that there never was a time when he didn't long to know his father on different terms, in spite of the rage, the hate, and the pain. *Time works you over,* he thought. *Time throws coal on what pisses you off and keeps it burning or cools it with water, making you think you're in control. Either way,* he thought, *you don't forget. You live with the conflict.*

CJ's journey became intertwined with Loretha's in 1973. By that year, his tour in the Peace Corps was a fond memory. He had completed medical school and was a practicing physician. Dolores had completed graduate studies and was a social worker. They were working with the rural poor in Alabama, when CJ received a letter from his mother, Lovely Bernard, telling him she had cancer and needed to see him, needed him to take charge of her affairs.

He joined the staff at the General as soon as he got back to town, and he thought the decision was one of convenience—safe, ordinary, wise. It was a ritualistic given that he'd do that. All black doctors coming through town did time at the General before branching into private practice or some high-paying specialty. The General always needed doctors, and he needed to make some money while he took charge of his mother's life. Had he known just how much the General would shake up his universe, perhaps he would have looked for other options.

Lovely was alone in the oversized house he'd grown up in on the upscale side of town, where many of the General's doctors lived. For years they were the only black folks living in the area. When CJ was a boy, he'd overhear his father bragging about how he tricked his way into getting the property. If you pressed him though, he'd admit having help from a few white friends who fronted for him with the real estate agents.

But by 1973, about the only people going in and out that house were the domestic workers who'd ride over on the bus from Desert Haven, the visiting nurses, and a few of Lovely's friends who took turns running errands for her.

His mother finally divorced his father when CJ was in medical school. It wasn't because she didn't love him anymore, CJ knew that. She did. She just wanted to guarantee that all of her worldly goods would go to her son, Clay Jr., after her death.

He reasoned that she had another motive too. She didn't want any of her money to filter its way to his father's girlfriends. So if she needed someone to manage her personal affairs as she approached the end of her earthly time, it would be her son. He had her trust as no other did. When he arrived back at his old home, he found his mother sitting in front of the bay window, looking out, so she could watch him walk toward the house.

"Where is she?" Lovely said, after they'd hugged and kissed and he felt the sickness in her.

"She who?" he asked, looking her over, then picking up a bottle of pills from a side table next to her chair.

"Be my son right now, not my doctor."

They hadn't seen each other in almost two years. When he had finished medical school, he flew home briefly before going to Alabama to work in the evolving and sometimes faltering civil rights movement, but as a doctor, not as a street fighter.

"You know who I'm talking about, Clay Jr. She pregnant?"

He placed the bottle back on the table, frowned, and turned his head slowly toward her. He felt relief to see her grinning at him. He knew though, that through her playfulness, she meant it. She was looking for something to leave behind besides a big house and a few bank accounts. She wanted the assurance of love in her son's life and wanted to see his likeness in a grandchild. Her nagging started when he first wrote home and mentioned Dolores.

"She's anxious to meet you too, Mom," he said.

During the first few days after returning to California, CJ tried to call his father several times, but the number was not in service. He figured his father was still part owner in a medical lab across town, so CJ made a mental note to drop by the lab one day after leaving the hospital, but that thought held no urgency. Still, he'd be able to tell Lovely he tried, knowing sooner or later she'd ask if he'd talked to him. He was aware his father was involved in some research up at the General too, and he wondered what the reaction would be if they ran into each other.

CJ's ending up with Loretha's medical chart, along with a stack of others, started as a mildly important event. Dr. Jenkins liked to call him Young Dr. Bernard, and she told him one day that it would be a good idea if he took on some of the patients in the arthritis research project. The health of a few had started to decline, and she could use his help to figure out why. He saw no reason not to go along with her enthusiasm over his being at the General, so he accepted, thinking it would give him another reason to intensify the search for his father.

But then Dr. Jenkins let him know something else. It wasn't just that the patients were getting sick. They didn't have a chance to talk with Dr. Bernard before he left and they seemed quite upset.

"How is he? Better I hope. Such a shock, his leaving so suddenly."

CJ rolled his tongue around in his mouth, looked away and nodded before speaking. He didn't want to let on that this was the first he'd heard about his father being sick.

"Thanks for asking. He's getting on as well as can be expected."

"Well, I am glad. And seeing you may be just what's needed to put those patients at ease."

Not wanting to dodge any more questions, he thought of an excuse and hurried away from Dr. Jenkins. He figured Lovely didn't know about his father's illness either or else she'd have mentioned it, and if anyone in her circle knew, they were keeping the news from her. He asked himself whether he should tell her and then decided against it. He'd wait until he had more information. No sense in giving her a reason to worry. The idea that his father's health could be a problem didn't initially alarm him. Instead, he was quietly seething because he'd been shut out again. Not even illness was of any of his business.

The news from Dr. Jenkins sent CJ searching for his father once again. But her words had to cut through his anger first. The thought that both his folks could be sick at the same time is what did it. How was he going to take care of two sick people? Maybe his father still had another woman, someone who'd stand by him through thick and thin, the way Lovely once did until she just couldn't take any more.

CJ's problem was where to begin looking, because it occurred to him that since his folks divorced, the only address he had for his father was a post office box. So he started there with a short note.

Sir, I'm in town taking care of Mom, on staff at the General too. Are you okay? What's going on? Call me at the house, please. Clay Jr.

The day the note returned unopened and marked "No forwarding address" by the post office, CJ drove across town and into the eastern edge of Desert Haven where his father's medical lab was located.

Even before he stated his name, the look on the receptionist's face told him that his father's affairs at the lab were troubled.

"I'm Clay Bernard Jr."

"Yes, I see," said the woman, before he finished his sentence.

"Well," said CJ, clearing his throat. "I'd like to speak with my father, if I may, or leave a message."

"Dr. Bernard is no longer affiliated with this lab," she said.

CJ exhaled, his look revealing his disappointment. He stared at the woman for a moment while questions formed in his mind and he settled on one to ask.

"When was the last time ...?"

"I really don't know what to tell you, Mr. Bernard."

"Doctor Bernard," CJ said, looking down and then up before allowing his eyes to meet hers again. "Well," he said, struggling to recover his composure, "if you hear from him again, would you tell him I need to speak with him?"

Chapter 17

"How come Dad doesn't like us? I mean he's always mad." CJ was twelve when he put this question to his mother. He asked during Sunday dinner. He asked because he couldn't remember the last time his father ate dinner with Aunt Pearlie, his mother, and him. It was the one weekly meal they had together and he missed him, even though being around him was just as painful. He really meant to ask why he didn't come home much anymore, but the unintended questions, the ones really on his mind, came out of his mouth.

"You ought to be ashamed of yourself, Clay Jr.," his Aunt Pearlie said. "Back in my day, you'd have gotten a good beating for even thinking something like that."

Clay stopped listening to his Aunt's complaints about his behavior whenever his father wasn't around, after he figured out the main reason she lived with them. It was to be his surrogate mother, standing in for Lovely, a nurse at a private hospital.

"After dinner, Clay, we're going to have a talk," Lovely said.

He hated those talks almost as much as he hated the riveting stares he'd get from his father—unblinking, unwavering, cold stares. He hated how she made him feel guilty for doubting his father too. He'd shut his mouth to turn off the guilt, every time.

"You're nothing but a momma's boy, aren't you?"

Clay would try not to speak when his father asked that question, but the elder Bernard would demand an answer.

"What ... answer me boy. Cat got your tongue?"

"No, sir."

"No, sir, what?"

"No, sir. I'm not a momma's boy."

That question always signaled a beginning, like an introduction to a torrent of words measuring him against some rules that weren't written down anywhere. The rules existed only in his father's mind, reserved just for him, Clay Jr. Sometimes, CJ got more than harsh words. He'd be forced to follow his father to the basement, where the words were punctuated with the slap of a belt across his back.

But he learned to endure the abuse in relative silence. He refused to cry, at least not in front of his father. He wouldn't cry in front of his mother either. He'd go to his room or into the backyard citrus grove, and cry and mentally beat his father up in private.

He knew she'd find him though, for one of her talks. He could make it a conversation if he liked. Lovely would let him, give him room to express himself, and talk out some of the rage and fear burning in him. She'd even nudge him, but after being stripped naked and whipped by his father's hard stare, harsh words, and leather belt, all he could do was roll with the waves of shame he felt, and Lovely's nudging would just make things worse. She'd whisper things to him about his father that didn't make sense, things that didn't match what CJ saw and felt.

"He's hard on you, Clay Jr., but he loves you. Never forget that."

I don't need his kind of love, he thought.

"It's his way of making sure you grow up strong. You'll understand when you get older, and you'll be more like him than you think."

No, I won't, he thought. *I hate him.*

He was eighteen when he quit being guilty for good and started referring to his father as his old man. It was after Aunt Pearlie lost her footing, slipped, and broke a couple of her fragile bones. By then she'd ceased being the one caring for others and needed people around to care for her. Lovely called an ambulance and told CJ to drive over to the country club, look for his father, and tell him to meet her at the Westgate Memorial Hospital.

That was a reasonable plan in CJ's mind, but when he got to the club, he decided to drive around the parking lot looking for his father's silver sports car before asking if anyone had seen Dr. Claymore Bernard. He never did see the car, but he did see him. His back was turned, and he seemed to be hunching over slightly. CJ could tell someone was standing in front of him. He stepped on the gas and sped toward them, pulling close enough so he could be heard as he yelled out the window. But his father yelled at him first.

"Clay Jr., slow down. What are you doing here anyway?"

There was a woman with him, and Clay Jr. drove up just in time to see them quickly pull away from each other.

"Mom's at Westgate with Aunt Pearlie."

His father yelled at him again for not calling the clubhouse first, and CJ received no sympathy when he said he was just following his mother's instructions.

"Sorry for interrupting," he said, turning his eyes away and pretending to ignore the woman.

"Tell your mother I'll be there shortly," his father said as CJ began driving away.

"Yes, sir," he said. "Old man," he mumbled.

CJ sped off, deliberately not slowing down when he turned from the parking lot and onto the street. He didn't exactly see them kissing but didn't have to. In his mind he'd caught his father playing around. And he had been yelled at in front of a stranger. Now he knew why his father didn't want Lovely or him stopping by the club without calling first. He conjured up a familiar fantasy as he headed to the hospital, the one where he stood up to his father, told him off, and left to live on his own. He wondered even back then how much his mother knew.

"I couldn't find him," he said to Lovely.

His father never did make it to Westgate.

A part of CJ actually welcomed Dr. Jenkins's gesture. He found a table in the physicians' lounge where he could sit and read, thinking all the while how ironic that he'd get a different view of his father from studying his scribbles on medical charts. He read the records carefully and noted that all the patients had minor surgery a month after signing up. And he wondered why new patients were brought into the project at the beginning of that year, 1973, especially since that's when the research team began noticing unexpected changes in the health of some patients. Was a phase of the project ending and a new one starting? How could that be?

He wrote a note to himself to ask Dr. Jenkins about it. He thought it must have been a mistake, and these new patients were ones his father saw in the main clinic.

He looked for warnings on Loretha's chart and saw notations about when her symptoms began changing. The date on one note was June 3, 1970. In the early stages, up to 1966, the drug administered was Aurosyn. Later, in 1967, the name changed to an abbreviation and a number, CEB3XX, and he couldn't figure out why. He recognized the first drug as one on the market since the late sixties, so he asked himself some questions. Why was the second drug introduced? Why hadn't he read about this CEB3XX in the medical literature? What pharmaceutical company produced it?

He expected some of his father's former patients to be surprised to see him, but Loretha seemed hostile, and he wondered if she and his father had had a falling out. She looked at him as if she didn't believe her eyes, and he sensed she wanted to say something but held it in. Finally, she shook his hand, saying his name at least three times, and she didn't smile at all during the time they were together.

"I see you're having some setbacks with the arthritis," he said.

He proceeded to gently press the sides of her neck just under the chin, checking her glands and then her ears and nasal passages. He checked her heartbeat and lungs and told her he was ordering new lab work. All the while, he sensed her straining to either place him in her world, or to expel him from it. He advised her to see a social worker, even wrote a referral to help her deal with all the changes she was going through. Although she didn't respond, he told her he'd make sure someone from social services would contact her in a few days.

Loretha's look, though unnerving, was familiar. He'd seen it dozens of times. Women in pain wore it like a mask to control their anguish, to muffle their moans. He'd seen that look on the faces of Ghanaian women struggling with hard childbirth and tropical maladies they couldn't shake, and on the faces of poor women in the Alabama backwoods, women with cuts, scrapes, and boils that wouldn't heal. But as he observed more closely, exchanged wordless glances with them, or heard their stories, he'd come to see their expressions as not masks at all but as stark truth, staid looks of courage.

"What?" they seemed to convey to him. "I am strong. What have you brought me? Hope? Relief? Or more misery? Tell me. Bring it to me whichever it is, so I can fold it into my truth."

Chapter 18

On his walk along the beach that first night in Puerto de Vida, CJ reflected on the summer of '74 when he and the rest of the city discovered what his father had done. The truth was that CJ had nowhere else to go when the news broke, yet to his credit, running away wasn't even in his head. He knew he was being called into a fight, and his instinct was to step up.

The General placed him on unpaid leave after Loretha's flier made it all the way up to the hospital board. It happened fast and it perplexed him. He expected to be questioned, but he didn't expect to be punished for his father's actions.

"Dr. Bernard, where is your father?" asked the General's chief administrator.

CJ told him he didn't know. He and his father hadn't been on speaking terms for a while, but it was clear the administrator didn't believe him. CJ became more and more annoyed with all the questions hurled his way, and he regretted giving up as much information as he did.

At first he couldn't quite understand why he felt protective toward his father, why he didn't just tell the administrator that Claymore Earnest

Bernard, Sr., had disappeared, and no one knew where he'd gone or even if he was still alive.

Even Dr. Jenkins treated CJ differently. He approached her about the drugs his father gave to human research subjects, and she treated him like he had a disease she didn't want to catch. She knew, and maybe she was the one who blew the whistle. He figured that in her eyes, he must have looked guilty by virtue of family ties. His father carried out clandestine research using poor people, and since he was a doctor too, he must have known, must have been just as tainted.

Anyway, he couldn't leave town because of Lovely, and no other hospital would employ him under the circumstances. There were people at the General though who must have suspected long before Dr. Jenkins and he figured things out. They just didn't have the guts to go up against the respectable Dr. Bernard, and worse yet, somebody there had to be in it with him.

CJ thought for a minute. Dr. Jenkins might have been part of the scheme and joined the chorus placing blame on his father in order to deflect suspicion away from herself. Then just as quickly, he backed away from that thought. It didn't feel right. Dr. Jenkins was clean and righteously indignant.

For CJ, the whole thing rolled up into an unmistakably clear truth. He was forced out of the General, but he had no desire to back away from the trouble facing him. He had to do something for all those people his old man had hurt. That's where he'd enter the fight.

He'd heard when death is closing in on someone, their intuition sharpens. Maybe that's what happened to Loretha, or maybe her intuition was sharp all along.

"Where's your daddy?" she asked him that day in the coalition office when he showed up unannounced and unexpected, looking for her.

When she asked, Solly stood close enough for CJ to hear him breathing.

"I don't know where he is."

"How come you're not with him?"

The people in the office, already quiet, got even quieter. The foot shuffling stopped; the throat clearing ceased.

"He doesn't want me with him, and what he did is ruining my name right along with his."

Loretha, who had been standing with her back against the wall and her arms folded across her chest, left the wall and sat down.

"Tell me what I've got," she said.

CJ sat across from her and leaned forward, resting his arms on his knees. He blew air from his mouth like smoke from a cigarette and felt a little calmer when Solly moved around to sit next to her.

"From 1964 to 1969, you were treated with an experimental drug, Aurosyn, specifically for arthritis. Your surgery back in '64 was to place a tiny sac filled with the drug into your knees. The sac was supposed to release small amounts of the drug over time before dissolving into your bloodstream. Meanwhile, you received small doses of the medicine to take by mouth daily. In '69, Aurosyn was approved and hit the market as a prescription drug in pill form. The implant was never approved. The sac was made of a cancer-causing synthetic substance that poisoned your bloodstream. Between '69 and '73, you were given two more experimental drugs, I suspect, to counteract the harm the sac caused, but those drugs could not undo the damage. You have cancer, Miss Emmitt. That's why you are in so much pain."

"Your daddy ought to go to jail for what he's done," she said.

Her words burned his insides. He flushed. It had been a long time since he felt so much shame, and usually it was his father making him feel that way. It was the kind of feeling that made him want to lash out at the person delivering the punch. And he was angry toward Loretha for voicing what he couldn't bring himself to say, that his father was a criminal. He swore at Claymore Earnest Bernard, Sr., for not being there to face Loretha's stare and feel the sting of her words.

"I'm sorry for what he did to you and all the others."

He sat motionless, still leaning forward, looking at Loretha for a long moment. What she asked him next exposed and blocked him at the same time, like he had run into a large rock in the current of incidental events and couldn't see how to navigate around it.

"Why do you hate your daddy?"

His mouth opened slightly. He was trying to hold in shock, and her question only added to his feeling of shame. Then he leaned back, symbolically putting distance between them.

"That's personal. Why does it matter to you?"

"Because," she said, "if you're still going to be my doctor, you can't be bringing hate with you to my treatments."

"Are you saying you don't hate him?"

"I'm saying I don't want to leave the world with hate all built up inside. I'm working on mine. What are you going to do for yours?"

Before that moment, it hadn't occurred to CJ to do anything with his feelings about his father. He was as accustomed to them as he was to Claymore Earnest Bernard Senior's coldness.

Loretha's appeal to the hospital board got the district attorney listening. He announced at a press conference that he'd convene a grand jury, and members of the hospital board as well as Dr. Claymore Bernard would be subpoenaed. Looking back at how fast events moved that summer, CJ suspected the district attorney had been alerted even before Loretha confronted the board. What he was absolutely sure of from that moment forward was that his old man didn't leave the General because he was sick. He left on the run from what he'd done.

That summer too, Lovely died a day after she learned about the scandal from the evening news. The day she heard, CJ helped her out to the back patio so they could enjoy dinner in the evening warmth, and she could look out at the acre array of flowers and fruit trees she loved. Once she told him there were two things she would miss when she died, that garden and him. She was lighthearted when she said it and so they laughed. CJ thought she was surprisingly calm given all the publicity about his father. He decided not to talk about it unless she did. They finished their dessert, and CJ started on a glass of after-dinner wine when she brought it up, the subject that had been leaning silently into them all evening.

"A sip of that wine sure would be nice," she said.

"You've got to take your medicine."

"A little bit won't hurt. At least it'll make me feel good. That's more than I can say for the medicine."

He emptied the last of the tea from her cup onto the grass and poured a little wine into it. She took a sip and looked at him.

"You feeling good now," he joked.

"Your father is in the worst trouble of his life," she said.

"Yeah, it sure seems like it."

He deliberately looked away toward the trees and flowers he knew the names of from spending time in that garden with her and Aunt Pearlie as he grew and as the plants grew, the lemon and orange trees lined in neat rows, stretching the length of the yard. Together with the flowering crape myrtle, the hyacinth, and the carefully arranged step gardens of rainbow-colored blooms, they created a landscape worthy of an artist's attention.

"Have you talked with him since you've been back?"

He waited again before answering, looking for words that conveyed the truth without hurting her further, then decided there were none.

"No. I can't find him. No one can. He hasn't been seen in months, not even at the medical lab."

CJ figured her response would be slow in coming forth. She always looked for a way to defend his father and find excuses for his behavior. He wondered if this news would show him something different about Lovely. It didn't.

"Your father wanted to make his name in medicine ... to prove he's just as good as anybody else. Colored doctors always had to do more, know more than anybody else. Always had to prove themselves. I watched him get more and more bitter year after year. He wouldn't hurt all those people on purpose, Clay Jr., you have to know that ... a name for himself, that's what he wanted."

CJ kept right on looking into the distance, sipping his wine.

"He's still got some goodness in him, you know. You shouldn't give up on him."

He could feel her watching. Her illness seemed to heighten her capacity to stare into him, especially when she was intent on planting ideas in his mind the way she once placed seeds in the ground and watered them, talked to them, and coaxed them to give her their beauty.

"Promise me you won't," she said.

He waited before speaking, holding the wine in his mouth, passively judging its flavor while he delayed his reply. He didn't want to make such a promise.

"I'll think about it, Mom," he said.

He waited again.

"For many years, I thought about leaving him, but—" she said, motioning for him to put more wine in her cup. When he refused, she slumped back in the chair. "I couldn't, and it wasn't because I'd lose my social status as a doctor's wife. I just kept looking for the reason he changed."

"Mom, the war changed him. Remember how you used to tell me that?"

"I know," she said. "Something about that war got deep down inside him. He came back defiant, driven, and even reckless at times. I always felt if I could get at the root of it all, get him to talk about what happened over there, the Claymore I fell in love with would reappear."

"War takes away more than the eye sees," CJ said, finally looking at his mother.

Lovely nodded and frowned as she sipped the last drop of wine left in her cup.

The next morning he found her breathing but unconscious and cold to the touch. He called the ambulance, and while he waited for help, he called Dolores.

"This is it, Dee," he said. "I don't think she'll live through the day."

Lovely died shortly after arriving at Westgate Memorial. Before she exhaled her final breath, he gave her the promise she wanted, and he thought as he spoke that she knew all along it was the last request she'd ask of him. He knew she could hear him and he trusted his words were comforting, but he hoped that the life force leaving her body couldn't read his thoughts. He was silently cursing his father and holding out on what not giving up meant, like it was a wild card from an obscene deck. *Give up?* CJ thought. *Why shouldn't I give up? All those times he used to beat the crap out of me. Make me a man, he said. What kind of man is he for running? Why should I care?*

The big, cathedral-like Baptist church in Desert Haven that Lovely attended practically every Sunday for years was packed with mourners for her funeral. All through the service, CJ was at war with an impulse to watch for his father. He stared at the faces of long-time family friends for signs that they knew his father's whereabouts and were keeping secrets.

Not able to read deception on their faces, he turned his attention to the preacher's benevolent and humorous stories about Lovely and listened to her sorority sisters eulogize her. He forced himself to focus on the side view of her still body at rest in its silk-lined casket. Then he commanded the specter of his father to go away. If Claymore Earnest Bernard Senior was too afraid to show up for Lovely's funeral, CJ didn't want him occupying space in his head.

But the command collided with his thoughts about Lovely's last request. The words "Get out of my head" and "Don't give up" circled around the vision of his father's face, and CJ let out a loud sob. He leaned forward as Dolores caressed his neck and shoulders as people do at funerals when comforting the bereaved. She touched him just when a wave of grief rumbled from him and became a shout.

"He ought to be here, Lovely. How come he's not?"

After the burial, Dolores convinced CJ to file a missing person's report, and she drove to the police station with him to make sure he didn't change his mind. She told him at least he could do that much to honor his promise to Lovely.

"That sorry old man should have been at the funeral," CJ said.

"But what if something's happened to him? We just don't know, CJ."

He inherited the property, but had no intention of living in that house any longer than necessary to sell it. Dolores didn't return to Alabama; instead she settled in with him and helped decide what to keep and what to list in the estate sale. It was she who found a collection of letters and photographs

Lovely had kept locked in a desk drawer in her bedroom.

CJ looked through them and saw that the earliest ones were from his father to Lovely, written during the war years. As he removed them from the envelopes, he again noted the irony of his actions, that he was about to glimpse into the mystery of his father by reading his ramblings on letters Lovely treasured. He wished he'd found the letters earlier and buried them with her.

But there was a stack of letters dated after the war that were addressed to his father from someone in England. The letters spanned years, and there were photographs of some people with names CJ couldn't recall ever hearing his father mention. The last was dated in 1960. He and Dolores wondered why the letters were in Lovely's possession, why she held on to them. He sat on the floor at the foot of her bed and began reading. By the time he finished, he knew why. That summer night, neighbors saw smoke coming from the Bernard's chimney. CJ burned the letters.

Dolores tried to talk him out of burning all of them. She tried to convince him to save the photographs, but CJ's grief had slung again into rage, and she was glad Lovely and his father weren't around to witness it.

Three months later, CJ and Dolores got married in a simple civil ceremony, because she was pregnant with Lovely's grandchild.

Part IV

᪥

September 1977
Coming Forth by Day

Chapter 19

On the third night of the *carnaval*, the travelers from Desert Haven gathered on the beach to watch the final pageantry of Califa's mystery play out as a light show on the ocean. They took food, drink, blankets, and canvas chairs down with them. They collected wood and debris, piled it high for a fire so the flames lit the faded gold veneer of Califa's wooden statue that had stood silent on the beach for years. It was their way of showing respect for the myth that sustained the people of Puerto de Vida.

It was Loretha's idea, spending the last night near the water instead of perched on the hillsides along with all the other tourists, wrapped in blankets and holding lanterns. She wanted to be alone with her companions, maybe for the last time. She didn't know. She wanted to tell them how free she felt when she opened up, came forth, stepped from the oppression of her secrets.

She saw, even before they arrived in Puerto de Vida, that her companions were working overtime to appear in control. And at the *carnaval*, they worked just as hard to hide their uncertainties by being loud, drinking and eating too much, and acting out with abandon as if they didn't know when they'd have that much fun again.

Loretha was in top form that final night. Somebody in her physical condition was supposed to be barely moving and talking slowly, halfway in this world and not quite in the next. She was none of that. She felt sizzling with life, and the feeling had been building for three days. Her friends noticed too, and seeing her that way was a relief, giving them further excuse to act out. They uncorked more wine bottles, church-keyed beer cans, and obligingly unscrewed the cap from a jug of cider for Loretha, Dolores, and Malakia. The men told jokes at each other's expense and seemed to be in a contest to see who could be the most outrageous. The women laughed at some of those jokes and rolled their eyes at others. But no one called all that playing around to a halt. Loretha wondered if she'd be able to break through, to get them to trust each other with their secrets without stopping the fun.

After settling on the small patch of sand they'd claimed, they looked around and saw that they'd created a makeshift village, with the women and child in the center and the men on the perimeter, carousing, yes, but mindful. The arrangement comforted all of them in a primitive, tribal way, and Loretha began to feel that the setting was just right for her to summon her nerve and open up once more.

Solly, CJ, and Roy took off their flip-flops, rolled up their pant legs and wandered toward the ocean. With wine and beer containers in hand, they looked at a ball of light hovering near the horizon.

The hillside onlookers watched and pointed, saying it was Califa's chariot gliding on the water.

Under the influence of the full moon and frequent trips to her own special Sangria canteen, Professor Howard's mood had visibly changed, and she began staring at Califa's statue and calling her name. She sat on the ground facing it, with her back to the fire and everyone else. Loretha, quietly listening to Dolores as she tried to sing Malakia to sleep, watched Professor Howard's actions, and after a few minutes of steadily gazing at her back, whispered her name.

Professor Howard answered by turning her whole body sideways and fixing her eyes on Loretha. She couldn't have heard the whisper, so it had to have been the gaze that disturbed her thoughts. Her expression asked a question. She wanted Loretha to show some compassion, like she did that night years ago when they grieved together about Marcus.

Professor Howard rolled over, propped up one knee for leverage, and then lifted herself upright. She trudged slowly through the sand toward Loretha and Dolores, holding a small black case under her left arm close to her heart, the way a lot of sanctified folks clutch their Bibles when they leave home and head for church.

Sucking sporadically on a pacifier, Malakia whined herself to sleep, with her mother's humming in the background. Dolores was finally free to join Loretha and Professor Howard in the talk of grown women. Their good time was subdued, however, for each had secrets on her mind about the men in her life, heavy loads troubling their private waters, and they intuitively felt some of their load would lighten before long.

Professor Howard squatted and sat next to Loretha. The women formed a tight triangle with Malakia wrapped snugly in blankets in the center. The fire at their backs threw enough light on the statue to send its shadow up the side of the rocks behind it, causing it to appear like a totem built to protect them.

"New baby due soon?" Professor Howard asked, letting the small black case slide down her side to the ground.

"December, ma'am, early I hope, before Christmas."

Even when Professor Howard slipped into her persona as Earth Momma, she was known to correct people if they called her ma'am. This time was different, for she settled into silence after hearing Dolores's answer. Loretha realized then that Professor Howard didn't come with them on that journey, not even surreptitiously. She wasn't crouching in the shadows. She was gone, but Earth Momma, usually jovial and feisty, mirrored Professor Howard's troubles all over her face.

"If I could, I'd be like that old gal over there," she said, pointing to Califa's statue. She grunted, frowned, and then laughed and turned the canteen up to her lips for a long swallow of wine.

Dolores gently moved Malakia closer and secured the blanket over her ears. Earth Momma looked her way and at the bundled-up child.

"Take good care of that child, you hear? Hold her. Let her know life is a come-as-you-are situation. Help her to be herself."

"Yes, ma'am."

Earth Momma opened the case and removed the photograph of Marcus, the one of him standing next to his grandfather's old Buick, and held it up.

"Look in his eyes," she said. "My papa tried to tell me what was in those eyes, but I didn't believe him. I might not ever see my boy again."

"You will if you let Roy help you." Loretha said.

Earth Momma looked at the men, who had started walking slowly back toward the women and the fire. Her eyes settled on Roy.

"Roy and Marcus, they never got close," she said.

"Why?" Loretha asked. "Why?"

Earth Momma's eyes moved from the men to the photograph and back to Loretha. The firelight made the tears trickling down her checks past her lips and chin appear red. She didn't bother to wipe them away.

"I guess because I wouldn't let them. Marcus lost so much. I didn't want him getting close to somebody he couldn't have. After my papa died, I tried to be everything to Marcus. Roy? After a while, he just let me be."

Dolores, listening closely, made a noise, a click of her tongue against her palate and a loud sigh.

"The missing," she said, leaning toward Loretha and Earth Momma. "My daddy-in-law is missing, maybe dead. 'Don't give up on your father,' CJ's momma told him. He doesn't know what that means, and I swear, he hates his father ... won't even say his name. Old man, that's what he calls him."

She looked back over her shoulder at the men. They'd stopped walking when they reached the ice chest and were busy removing more beer and wine.

She hurriedly turned to look at Loretha and Earth Momma again.

"CJ doesn't know this, but I check the obituaries regularly for news of his father, and he's not the only missing Bernard."

The men joined the women, with Solly squatting on the ground beside Loretha's chair and CJ on the blanket with Dolores. Roy retrieved two canvas chairs, unfolded one for Earth Momma and the other for himself.

"Why y'all get quiet as soon as we come back?" Solly asked. "Were you gossiping about us?" He laughed.

"Ha, that must be the reason my ears are burning," Roy said.

"We need to talk," Earth Momma said, loud enough for everyone to hear. She was speaking to Roy and had placed her hand on his knee. "Will you help me find Marcus?"

Roy glanced at Solly, but the look was not one of surprise. Then he placed his hand on Earth Momma's.

"Marcus needs to stay where he is awhile longer. It's not safe for us to go looking for him."

"You … you and Solly kept it from me," she said, in a near whisper. "You've known all along."

They all got quiet, letting the drama between Roy and Earth Momma absorb their attention. It was as if they needed time to figure out what to say. Loretha broke the silence.

"Solly, I've felt for a while that you helped Marcus disappear … just didn't know why … what trouble he was in … I could see the both of you … you know? Running, just running … then hiding.

That money in the desert, the bank robbery, was that why?"

Solly looked at her briefly, then turned his eyes away, leaving her question unanswered. But she kept looking at him, searching his profile for more clues, more messages about the truth. His manner of looking away reminded her of their argument years ago when he held steadfastly to silence and said it was to protect her. But now she was his wife, and she couldn't be forced to testify against him. Why is he holding out now? She asked herself.

"I hope everything works out all right for you, man." CJ said to Solly, once again breaking the quiet spell that had fallen over the village. He stood up as he talked, shaking his head as if he had made a decision and was about to reveal it.

"I don't know, can't be sure, but it seems like we're being called on by Loretha here to disclose things. Am I right?"

Loretha thought she heard quivering in his voice, and so did everyone else, because they all turned to look at CJ, and found his eyes filling with tears. He held a can of beer in one hand and a plastic cup of wine in the other, and he began to pour the wine on the ground.

"I learned in Ghana to offer a libation to the ancestors. So I am spilling this wine in honor of my mother, Lovely Bernard. May she rest in sweet peace."

He dropped the cup to the ground, spit into the beer can and held it up to the sky. "Here's to you, Dr. Claymore Earnest Bernard. May you rest in peace too, but I'm glad your bones aren't anywhere near my mom's." Then he walked a few feet away from their encampment and poured the beer onto the sand, crushed the can in his hands, and threw it as far as he could toward the ocean.

"He ran off to Georgia. They found him in a Motel 8 with a bullet in his head," CJ said, taking his seat again beside Dolores.

"CJ, why didn't you let somebody know? Why didn't you tell us?" Loretha and Dolores said, almost in unison.

"That's got to be eating you up, man," Solly said.

"Why? Why?" CJ questioned. "I'm pissed off with him that's why. He shamed the family ... and he didn't love us, me, my mom ... or my brother."

"After the war Dr. Bernard left a son in England," Dolores said. "I've tried to get CJ to contact his brother, but he won't."

That's who I saw, Loretha thought, remembering the rally in MLK Park and the man she imagined standing near CJ. He has a brother. That recollection triggered a sensation in her, like warm water flowing upward against gravity from her womb to her heart. She looked at Solly and her stare was so blank, it startled him. She looked away, raised her head, sighed, and spoke.

"CJ's brother is waiting for him to call, and Solly is waiting for me to make my move. When I die, he's running, just like Marcus did. But it's okay 'cause, you know the old saying, life is for the living, and Solly, you've got to survive as long as you can, any way you can. I wanted us to be alone on the beach tonight so I could unload on all of you. Let you know how good I feel about not having any more secrets ... how good I feel about having you as family ... 'cause really, you are all I've got. But you ... you let loose and dumped so much pain on

242

this beach, all we can do now is let it go, forgive, and let the water wash it away."

If eyes from above and from the cliffs and the ocean were watching that night, they'd have seen six grown folks and a sleeping child make their way to the place where the water caressed the land. There they stood. They talked, revealing more long-held secrets. At times they fell silent, holding on, unsure of how much to speak. Then they hugged, kissed, and cried. And when they felt satisfied, they turned toward the east, headed back toward higher ground just as dawn was coming forth.

The End

9 781495 801396